The Darkness

In the Shadows

A Provocative Series by Tony Nalley
Based on a True Story

THE DARKNESS IN THE SHADOWS

THE DARKNESS IN THE SHADOWS

"Two young hearts are torn apart by the brutal actions of their Church's Youth Minister. One couldn't tell her secret, and the other couldn't know. Bound by a promise made to one another in a little church in Michigan, both of their lives are changed forever. When they are re-united years later …and their passions are rekindled, neither realizes just how distant their lives …and their very souls have become. Murder, mystery, romance, and witchcraft abound in this modern-day novel. It's a psychological drama with a paranormal twist."

T.N.

THE DARKNESS IN THE SHADOWS

from the author

The premise of this series is to create emotion within the reader. Too many times do we as a society, encompass depth of meaning into single solitary words, rape, sodomy, molestation. It is easier as a society to set aside the emotional trauma and lifelong repercussions inside a distinct and legal term or analogy and dismiss it once the perpetrator has been sentenced.

These acts of violence have far reaching ramifications that often change the psychological makeup of the victim; their lives, the lives of those around them …and their future lives. It alters the universal timeline and reality.

It is much easier to say that the criminal needs to be put away than to understand the seriousness and complexity of their actions. Because, if you were to see what happened, if you were allowed to peer into the mind of both the perpetrator and the victim, the criminal would not get off so easy with mere jail time. Their entrails would be burned, their bodies would be hung, and they would be buried in unmarked graves.

This series is a work of fiction, though many of the events are based upon factual occurrences. All names and locations have been changed to protect the innocent. And no emotional, spiritual, societal or physical harm is intended or implied.

These crimes never happened to me. But similar transgressions have happened to others around me.

The consequences were devastating. They have affected my life, and they have touched and changed countless other lives.

In many ways we are all connected. The air we breathe. The steps we take. The paths we choose are all intertwined.

Like a single drop of rain upon the water, what happens to one of us has rippling effects upon us all.

Tony

National Suicide Prevention Lifeline
Call 1-800-273-8255
Available 24 hours a day

National Child Abuse Hotline is available 24/7 at
(1-800) 4-A-Child or (1-800) 422-4453

National Sexual Assault Hotline
Call 1-800-656-4673
Available 24 hours a day

TONY NALLEY

♫ The world was on fire, and no one could save me but you. It's strange what desire will make foolish people do. I'd never dreamed that I'd meet somebody like you. And I'd never dreamed that I'd lose somebody like you. No, I don't want to fall in love. No, I don't want to fall in love with you. ♫

♫ What a wicked game you played to make me feel this way. What a wicked thing to do to let me dream of you. What a wicked thing to say you never felt this way. What a wicked thing to do to make me dream of you. And I don't want to fall in love. ♫ Wicked Game - Chris Isaak

...a foreshadowing

The soft sound of wind chimes filled the silence of the night as the breeze gently blew through the darkness, bringing with it the sweet aromas of flowers and a distant rain. Tommy sat on the cool stone porch with his bare feet dangling over the side into Tara's flower garden filled with white smooth stones. The moon had risen in the early morning sky and cast its light upon the grass in the night.

Tara noticed how the light spread its shadows through Tommy's unbuttoned shirt and outlined his distinctly masculine form ...as he sat below her and leaned lovingly upon her bare leg.

They had been sharing their souls and Tommy had been sharing his memories ...memories she didn't have ...or at least ones she didn't remember. He had spoken to her about a concert ...one he had taken her to the night of her car accident. Tara didn't remember going to the Rick Springfield concert or the opening bands that had performed. And she didn't remember being with Tommy sexually. But she remembered being dropped off in the Kroger store parking lot, and she remembered being left there alone.

And what Tara remembered vividly, was what had happened ...only moments after Tommy and his friends had left her there alone.

13

Chapter One – The Deafening Silence

As the boys left Tara sitting in the rusty old red Ford, and exited the Kroger store parking lot, Tommy and his friends were completely unaware of the dark and shadowy figure, which had been slowly slithering its way across the pavement.

It moved creepily and steadily; towards the Thunderbird she had gotten in to.

Tommy and his friends were drinking beer in their car, behind a line of others at a red-light a block away, while listening to loud music and honking their horns at pretty girls in other vehicles, before the shadowy snake finally reached her.

They had no idea they had left Tara, alone, at the gates of hell.

Suddenly.

Tara's car door opened with a loud noise and a screech of its hinges.

She was abruptly pulled out into the parking lot by her arm.

She heard shouting.

It was all happening so fast.

Someone was yelling at her.

"Oh my God." She panicked.

She recognized his voice. It was Dan.

"Stop it! Leave me alone!" She screamed. "Let go of me you fucker!"

He had been waiting for her. He had been stalking her.

He knew where she'd been. He had been watching.

Tara had placed herself in an extremely dangerous situation without any consideration for her own safety; his passions were insatiable, and his intentions were ravenous.

Dan held her tightly in the grip of his hand as he slapped and beat her face.

"You're a fucking little slut!" He shouted at her within full view and hearing distance, of the onlookers.

People in cars passed them by without stopping.

People on foot avoided her cries.

He smacked her face violently. He beat upon her leaving her badly bruised. He punched her in the stomach. And he pulled her hair, turning her face around to him so he could shout in her face.

Her bare legs and feet landed hard.

She'd scraped up her knees and legs, and she was bleeding.

Sitting on the cold blacktop, with the interior lights of the car on and with the door still wide open, Tara tasted the blood trickling from her busted lip.

"I need this!" Dan shouted as he reached down and picked her up.

Tara screamed and kicked and fought with him as he carried her back to his car. She was slobbering drunk and physically shaken, but she knew what he intended to do.

He had done it to her many times.

Dan had an insane look in his eyes. He had a wanting desire and a cannibal lust. His hands were shaking as he threw her in the front seat and slammed the door shut.

"You know I need this." He said as his heart thumped fast within his chest.

Tara positioned and prepared herself, in his passenger seat, for his unwanted advances. She didn't say a word as he reached for her, grabbing her hair, pulling her forward. She didn't dare to.

Tara was familiar with his movements, his sounds, knowing what he wanted, what he expected.

17

"Get in the backseat." He said through quivering and uneven breaths.

Tara quickly climbed over the seats and bounced onto the black faux leather in the back.

She had to do what he told her. She couldn't fight back.

She was drunk. He was too strong and too forceful. She had tried to fight him off, several times before, but he had only beaten her worse.

Dan had done unspeakable things. He had made her do unspeakable things.

He opened his car door, stepped outside in the Kroger parking lot and looked around to see if anyone was watching as he climbed in the backseat.

"Stop it, you bastard. You're hurting me!" She shouted openly.

"God, please make him stop!" She screamed out in her mind.

In her reactions to his intensity Tara scratched him deep with her fingernails.

Dan slapped her face brutally with the back of his hand.

Tara's head turned violently, and she screamed out in fright, as the pain and the force of his pressure took her breath.

Dan let loose his demons and he fed his sadistic appetite.

"Please don't Dan." Tara screamed. "Please stop. Please stop. Dan, please."

Dan placed his hands tightly and firmly around Tara's throat.

And he choked her.

Tara's body shook from her lack of oxygen.

She couldn't breathe.

Her body was convulsing.

She appeared lifeless, as she gagged and pleaded with her eyes for air.

With her body shuddering sporadically, Tara's mouth opened, exposing her tongue as she struggled and begged to stay alive.

Suddenly.

A rush of air.

A filling of lungs as Tara gasped the air in quickly.

19

As Dan looked out through the foggy backseat window, at the people who were walking back and forth from their cars to the grocery store, he looked down upon Tara's face.

"Babydoll," he said as she lay silently. Her eyes were swollen, and she faced away from him. "You know I love you, right? I never meant to hurt you, but you forced me to do this. This was your fault. You made me do this." He said condescendingly.

Moments later, she found herself being thrown from his car, and landing hard upon the pavement. She was badly beaten and bruised. As she hurriedly tried to dress herself upon the dimly lit asphalt, she heard Dan's engine roar loudly, as he tore out across the parking lot squalling tires, leaving her alone on the cold, hard and dirty black top.

She could hear whispers, mumbled voices of people coming from the shadows, but she could not see them.

Both of her eyes were now blackened and swollen shut, from his anger. And they stung from the pain like hellfire.

The pain came from her sweat and her tears …and her blood.

Tara forced herself to stand up and walk blindly across the darkened pavement. But this time, when she sat down inside her friend's car, she closed and locked the door.

20

She pulled her knees to her chest and wrapped her arms around them.

She was completely alone and confused. Everyone had betrayed her, even her own body. No one had called the police to report her attacker. No one had attempted to stop him from raping her. No one bothered to help.

Mamas walked with their babies' right beside her.

No one cared.

No one saw.

If they had, they turned away.

Beneath the shadows that lie and danced between the lights of oncoming traffic and streetlamps, Tara cradled herself and rocked back and forth amidst the gloom. And while she writhed in her severely emotional state of mind, her psychotic disillusion, she lost herself in the deafening silence within the darkness.

This was what Tara remembered. It was just hours before the car accident that would damage her spinal cord and place her in a wheelchair for the rest of her life.

Her cuts and bruises from the violent rape and abuse would be covered by the horrible cuts and bruises from the accident. And the injury to her back would supersede all other tests to be run and no one would ever know.

It was three-thirty-seven in the morning.

Tommy had listened to everything.

He stood up slowly from the cool back porch where he had been sitting, and he walked out into the darkness of the morning, where Tara could not see.

And he heaved, and he gagged, and he vomited in the grass.

TONY NALLEY

THE DARKNESS IN THE SHADOWS

Chapter Two – As You Wish

He hadn't slept all night.

The horrifying account of Tara's violent rape and suffering had left him in complete and total anguish.

It was sickening.

He was overwhelmed.

He was distraught.

"I did not know." He screamed in his thoughts as his pain showed upon his face. "I did not know."

He didn't know. And he was inundated with sickening and appalling visions, as he struggled with beleaguered remorse, shame and guilt.

He was nauseous. He was going to throw up again. So, he did.

He stood in the shower with the water running over his head for over an hour. It was her girls' bathroom. It was heavily laden with teenage bras and mascara, make-up, hair curlers and dryers. He felt dirty, being in there, where her children had dressed and undressed and had taken baths and showers themselves, and he didn't feel he would ever come clean enough.

"I could have saved her, if I'd had only taken her home that night." He screamed in his mind. "We could have been together. I could have stopped this."

His guilt was maddening.

"The past is in the past, Tommy." Tara said as she wheeled up beside him on the back porch and rubbed his back consolingly. "It wasn't your fault. I don't blame you. We can't re-write the past. We can't live in it. And we can't allow it to ruin the future."

Tommy grabbed her hand and pulled her arm over his shoulder, allowing her to hold him. And she did. She held him lovingly and reassuringly.

"For all of my life, Tara, all I have ever wanted, was for you to be happy and for you to be safe." He said. "When I found you in that church, in the arms of that man, I thought you were happy. I was a child. I was heartbroken, and I was devastated, and I did not understand." He spoke through tears. "How could anyone not love you?" He said as he looked into her eyes. "I have loved you since before I can remember. And I will love you, for every day of my life."

Tommy was openly weeping. And tears filled Tara's eyes.

They held each other as they slowly rocked back and forth. They could feel one another's heartbeat. His pulse became her pulse, his heartbeat; hers.

They sat together closely in silence, for a long while.

"You are the only one I've ever told." She related. "I've held it inside me, for all of my life."

It is inherently instilled in the genetic make-up and DNA of the male gender, to provide and protect those who are weak and more vulnerable. And when provided with an obstacle, a situation, whether emotional, physical or spiritual, instinctively, the male will attempt to provide restitution and resolution. But Tommy couldn't fix this.

"My heart, to your heart," Tommy said affectionately.

He had cut back. He was smoking less than a half a pack of cigarettes a day, while he had been around her. But since her morning revelations, he had already gone thru two whole packs and was opening a third. So, he lit up another one, and he sat back resting with his hands on the concrete porch behind him, and with his bare legs and feet crossed, upon the ground before him.

"We have always had a connection, you and I." Tommy said tenderly.

"A soul-tie." Tara responded.

"Yes, it's like no other I have ever known." He replied. "While I feel completely calm when we're together, simultaneously I'm also literally, on the edge of my seat." He said as he chuckled. "I am excited beyond all reason, while I'm also entirely at peace, tranquil and relaxed."

"I feel the same way." Tara related.

"It's fucking crazy." He said as he exhaled a deep breath of smoke.

The sounds of crickets, as they sang their songs, accompanied by the flashing yellow-green glow of lightening bugs, were uplifting. As he stood on the cool of the porch on his bare feet, he smoked, and he breathed in his feelings for her.

For Tommy, it had never been about having sex with Tara, it had been about their strong emotional bond, and their deeply spiritual connection. He had spent most of his life wondering if he had been the only one who felt it; wondering if she had felt it, too.

Tara watched the sun rise over the field as its light breached the darkened outline of trees in the distance. She didn't know how long this feeling of peace would last, so she embraced it fully. She breathed it in.

"Maybe I can …change." She thought. "Maybe my life can …change for the better."

"I'm making a list, Babe." Tommy said. "Spa, Elevator, Walk-in-tub, Rock-way to Guest house and fire-pit, Security locks and alarms, Plant trees, get pictures made, Rock-way paths to Angel tree, create website, Get EIN number and Business license, clean out Garage, storage shed and upstairs, Hot tub, Remember to Breathe, Laugh and Enjoy life."

"You just became my dream life-partner." Tara said excitedly. "You were damn close before, but now, it's a done deal."

"I also have magic hands. I love kisses and hugs." Tommy said. "And once the dust settles, you'll have a dream home."

"You have quite a range of vocabulary for being up all night." Tara laughed.

"You have no idea." Tommy laughed back.

Tommy had been tested when he was younger. He had scored very high on military tests given to him while in high school. They had asked him to join their military intelligence program once they had received his results.

But he had declined their offer.

He often downplayed his own IQ test scores. The average person's IQ score ranges between one-hundred, and one-hundred-twenty points.

Tommy's score was one-hundred-forty-six.

They told him that he was close to genius level.

It made him laugh.

"Once I was going to throw away a green-marbled trophy table, because it was unsteady, and it wobbled." He thought to himself. "It never occurred to me to get a screwdriver and tighten its screws." He laughed to himself. "I'm more than confident that I'm not a genius."

Tommy was very intelligent. And Tara found intelligence extremely attractive. Her husband, Michael, was also very intelligent. She assumed he was passed out upstairs from drinking all night in his room. She hadn't seen or heard from him all day.

"I made an appointment with the Real Estate agent to view the property this afternoon." Tommy said. "If you've got something else planned, I can reschedule with her."

Tara had lost herself in her thoughts of Michael, for a moment, just as Tommy had spoken about the land with the log cabins. She was remembering the times when they had been together intimately, when they had been good together.

She quickly refocused her thoughts and met his words with a smile.

"What time today?" She asked. "The only plans I have right now, are to get us some breakfast. I'm starving."

It was five minutes after seven in the morning. Tara drove.

As they found a corner booth, and the waitress brought their food, Tara sat Tommy's drink upon a folded napkin, and wiped off the water-ring his glass had left upon the table.

"You know," She stated. "I pursued my degree in psychology at the University to figure myself out."

Tommy cut his sausage with his fork, as he listened.

"I think I'm crazy, Tommy." She said seriously. "There is a darkness inside of me that I can't control. I know it's there because it clouds my mind and I have blackouts. I don't remember long periods of time, and when I'm told of things I've supposedly done, it scares me. It scares the hell out of me, Tommy."

Tommy reached out his hand and held hers tenderly.

"It takes a lot for me to tell you these things." Tara said as she squeezed his hand. "I want you to know that it means I trust you. Trust is above all other things, of the most value to me." She related. "I've taken you into my home and into the lives of my two girls, and I've even told Michael that you are going to be around regularly."

Tara sighed heavily and looked deeply into Tommy's eyes.

31

"I want you to help me write a letter to Dan." She said. "I want him to know that I remember and that I have survived."

Tommy had listened to her every word. He understood her fears. She hadn't spoken of her childhood sufferings or abuse to anyone, in all her life. She had kept her emotions bottled up inside her, since she was in the eighth or ninth grade, in junior high.

It had affected her entire life, her decisions, her interactions and her view of the world. And in the entire world, she had only placed her trust in him.

His friend, Seth, had suggested counseling. He believed she needed to speak with someone professionally, who had the wisdom and the knowledge to help her communicate her feelings, come to terms with the psychological trauma that she had endured, and possibly diagnose her dissociative identity disorder.

"As you wish," Tommy said as he squeezed her hand in return.

As you wish, means I love you.

It was a line from the Princess Bride. It was one of Tommy's favorite movies. Wesley was a farm boy who went abroad to seek his fortune at sea, to provide for his one true love. Anytime the girl asked him for something, his only reply was, as you wish. She was unaware of his meaning. She didn't understand that what he was truly saying was, I love you. Though, he had been saying it all along. When she finally comprehended his meaning, she realized that she loved him too.

Tommy was saying, I love you, but he was also saying so much more. Tara was his one true love. She had always been. For the first time since they had kissed under the lights of that Christmas tree, she was a part of him again.

He would help her write a letter to Dan. But he would also seek to land that bastard in prison for his actions.

And he would also speak with Tara about finding someone she could talk to, about the horrors of her childhood; someone with a solid professional background and knowledge.

"There is a light within you, Tara." Tommy told her. "You don't see it and I don't believe you are even aware. But within you is a light that is so bright, that it draws people to be near you."

"Like a bug light?" Tara said jokingly, as she made buzzing and zapping noises.

She laughed.

It was her way.

She thought it was funny.

"Did you know that I have an FBI record?" Tara interjected. "Yes, I was a reporter for the Washington Times, and I met with one of our more," Tara cleared her throat. "Shall I say, more sexually deviant Presidents? Anyway, he had placed his hand on my leg while taking a group picture. Afterwards, I remarked jokingly, and in my usual manner, that I had some of his DNA on me."

Tara laughed out loud.

"I was immediately escorted into a little closed off room, where I was interrogated by a swarm of FBI agents." Tara shook her head, yes. "True story, it was right after the Monica Lewinsky scandal broke."

Tommy shook his head.

"You know I've always had foot-in-mouth syndrome." She continued. "But that's why people love me."

Tara was a uniquely beautiful creature.

And then, Tommy thought of something funny, though, he didn't think it was the proper time to inform Tara of his extensive training in the fine and ancient arts of Sarcasm. Or that he had received the coveted Black-Belt from its use. He still thought it was funny.

And he didn't feel it was an appropriate time either, to discuss his well learned and wide-ranging knowledge, which had earned him a Bachelor-Degree in Pornography.

But he thought that was damned funny, too.

He chuckled to himself.

Chapter Three – Gentle on My Mind

He sat in the cool shade of a burgeoning oak, as the wind gently blew upon his skin, through his unbuttoned and opened blue long-sleeved shirt.

The scratch marks on his chest were clearly visible.

Susie and Bear lay flat upon the grass panting heavily beneath the timber, as Tara, Hope and Heather listened tentatively from the back porch beside him. Tommy played the strings of his Takamine guitar, and he sang one of his favorite country music songs, Gentle on My Mind by John Hartford.

♫ "It's knowing that your door is always open, and your path is free to walk, that makes me tend to leave my sleeping bag rolled up and stashed behind your couch. and it's knowing I'm not shackled, by forgotten words and bonds, and the ink stains that have dried upon some line, that keeps you in the backroads by the rivers of my memory that keeps you ever gentle on my mind." ♫

The music was mellow. Hope and Heather enjoyed it.

They hadn't expected to, because they listened to their own styles of music, from their own generation.

"He's got a great voice." Hope said surprisingly.

"Yes, he does." Tara agreed.

♫ "It's not clinging to the rocks and ivy planted on the columns now that binds me, or something that somebody said because they thought we fit together walking. It's just knowing that the world will not be cursing or forgiving, when I walk along some railroad track and find, that you are moving on the backroads by the rivers of my memory, and for hours you're just gentle on my mind." ♫

When he finished singing, Tommy laid his guitar down within its case, and he bashfully thanked the girls for their applause. He knew his limitations. He had performed in several bands. One of which had such a great lead singer, that he paled in comparison. But he was confident in his abilities and knew that at any given campfire surrounded by friends, family and other musicians, he would at least be in the top two or three.

"Have you ever heard of Grace Vanderwall?" Heather asked.

"Yes." Tommy answered. "I fell in love with her on AGT two years ago. She has amazing talent. And I respect her song writing abilities. In fact," Tommy continued. "Not only do I believe God is still creating angels because of her, but also, she reminds me of your mom when she was her age. She has the same way of captivating an audience and someone's attention just by her presence."

"Wow." Tara spoke up. "That was an extremely nice compliment, Tommy." She continued bashfully. "Thank you for that."

"Girls, do you know what I remember about your mom?" He asked. "Before the accident, your mama had the most attractive and seductive walk." He continued as his own face began to blush. "And wow. When she was wearing her tight blue-jean pants or those little purple shorts, God help any guy who stood behind her."

"You just told my thirteen and fourteen-year-old daughters, that their mama had a nice ass." Tara laughed.

"You did have a nice ass." Tommy said with a wink. "And so, help me God, you still do."

Heather was still uncomfortable with her mom openly flirting with another man, someone who was not her father. While she understood why, she still didn't think it was right, with her father still living at the house.

Though he'd spent most of his time upstairs, they were still married.

It didn't bother Hope. She wished everything were more out in the open. She didn't like to have to wait for the darkness in her mom to take over. She wanted to walk over to Tommy, pull it out, and suck him right then and there. She revered the scratch marks she had placed upon his chest, the night of their ritual. They were still prevalent. She had scratched him deeply.

39

She wanted to see her teeth marks, where she had bitten him.

Just then.

Tara's next-door neighbor drove up unexpectedly across the lawn. He was an older gentleman, whom she introduced to Tommy right away as Millard Jones, her best friend. He was driving a 4-wheeled all-terrain vehicle.

Millard was a kind looking old fellow, as he smiled and said hello. He lived next door, in a very nice home. His wife had died many years ago, and having no other family, he had emotionally adopted Tara and her two girls.

Heather and Hope jumped up and hugged him joyfully.

Heather liked Millard. Hope liked him, too. He had always been nice to their mom, and he had been like a grandpa to them both. He bought them presents for their birthdays and for Christmas. They were always fancy and expensive gifts.

The girls liked him a lot.

"Tommy, I hear good things about you from Tara and the girls." He said as he reached out his hand. "I also heard your guitar music. You're really good." He continued. "Would you like to take a ride and see my collections of fine bourbons and weapons? I have many rifles and pistols I think you might enjoy seeing."

"Sure. And thank you." Tommy said as he climbed in the passenger seat. "Would you girls mind looking after my guitar until I get back?"

"I will." Hope said calling first dibs.

Millard's home was immaculate. As Tommy was welcomed into the kitchen by way of the large, opened window-glass doors, he noticed the dark hardwood floors and the matching wood grains that adorned the kitchen's bar and the framed woodwork. The glass cabinets were trimmed in dark oak as well. It brought out the shine of the bourbon bottles and fine glasses they held within.

Throughout the living room, just off the pantry, the walls were adorned with rifles and eighteenth-century weapons encased in glass. Tommy remarked of how incredible his gun collection was and of how he also admired his collection of fine Bourbon and Scotch. Millard offered him a bottle of eighteen-year-old Buchanan's Scotch to take home with him.

Tommy gladly accepted.

Buchanan's eighteen-year-old Special reserve is a blend of grain and single malts that are married and then aged exclusively in ex-Sherry casks for a full eighteen years.

The flavor is a cross between Johnnie Walker Green and the Macallan twelve-year-old Scotch. The flavor is rich, almost decadent, and bold from the first sip.

"Tara and the girls mean the world to me." Millard said. "Don't hurt them, okay? They've been through a lot with Michael."

"I won't hurt them." Tommy replied. "I care about Tara very much. We've known each other since we were kids. I'm not here to hurt anybody."

"Good." Millard said. "I'll hold you to that."

Tommy walked back across the lawn, after parting ways with Millard, and seated himself on the porch beside Tara. He placed the Scotch bottle, tightly between his legs, as she stared solemnly across the fields of green.

"When the dust settles," Tara said as she ran her fingers through his hair. "I want you to move into the guest house. I know it's sudden, and I don't want to rush things, but it would be easier and better to have you close. Your son could live here, too." She suggested.

Tara had previously been a spokesperson for a marketing company, and she had been very successful doing so.

She became the face of the company's product to their customers. While traveling the country, she had digital photographs taken of her and her use of their products. She had also written about her use of the equipment as well as of their benefits. It had been a very lucrative endeavor. She had made six figures a year while enjoying what she did. And her business partner had made fifty thousand a year annually.

"Sadly, people in wheelchairs are not seen as attractive, or shown in a positive light, when they're smiling and happy." She related to Tommy. "I want to change that. And I want to help people see the opportunities they have, as well as help them make their lives better. That's why I want to buy some land as well, with fully accessible paths and log cabins." She continued. "I know we talked about this briefly, but it's also why I want you to partner with me in this business. You're a great writer. I'd love it if you were to join me."

"It sounds good to me. And I would enjoy writing with you and traveling." Tommy replied. "I'd have to discuss 'moving in' with my son. What about the girls? You can't just leave them here alone."

"I'd like to get them into modeling as well. They can be in photographs alone or with each other and can be a part of a family in certain situations." Tara stated. "They're both very photogenic, and this could become a rewarding family business."

"How soon do you want to begin?" Tommy asked.

"I'd like to start as soon as possible, obviously. But I still have the divorce to begin, and I need to have paperwork drawn up."

Tara ran her fingers across Tommy's chest and caressed his scratch marks.

"Who wants to eat Mexican?" She shouted.

Her girls came running quickly to the door.

"We do. We do." They both said excitedly.

"Get dressed quickly and meet us in the car." Tara told them.

Tommy rode shotgun as Tara drove them down the highway. She knew the roads well. And she took the curves and hills and bends along the one lane side road fast. The girls also knew the way, and they laughed as Tommy held on to the handle above his door.

In a few minutes they entered the Marion Springs City Limits.

"Mom." Heather yelled from the backseat. "We just passed a church sign. It was funny. Can we go back and get a picture?"

"Tommy, would you mind?" Tara asked him. "It's a scavenger hunt kind of game I've played with the girls for years."

"I don't mind at all." Tommy answered.

Tara turned the car around and they all looked for a church with a sign out front. They'd passed by two different churches before they found it.

"There it is." Heather shouted as she pointed up ahead.

Tara pulled the car to the curb as Heather and Hope got out and walked through the grass to the sign with their iPhones ready.

"TOO HOT TO CHANGE SIGN." The Christian church's sign read. "SIN BAD JESUS GOOD DETAILS INSIDE."

The girls had a good long laugh, after they had taken their pictures and jumped into the backseats.

While Tommy didn't find the humor in the words funny, he laughed. It never occurred to him that the sign's meaning could be changed completely with different placements of commas in the sentence.

They were kids. And this was an important communal game they played with their mom. Although it may have appeared, as something small, and insignificant to anyone else, it made him feel included, welcomed, and more a part of the family.

After having a wonderful meal at a Mexican restaurant located in downtown Marion Springs, they drove to meet the real-estate agent for the property they had discussed purchasing. It was a quarter mile off the main road and sat between rolling fields of grass across a small creek.

Two small, but beautifully built log cabins, stood on opposite ends of a large meadow upon adjacent hills. It would be impossible for Tara to see the woodland trails or traverse the open fields without assistance. Sadly, the owner's all-terrain vehicle needed repairs and wasn't capable of being driven.

But, with an old man's assistance, and with the strength of Tommy, Hope and Heather, Tara was able to see the inside one of the cabins. She was carried up a steep and wooden flight of stairs in her wheelchair, and she rolled easily through the closest of its barn-like cabin doors.

It was amazing inside and very well made. Its floors and walls were made of fine oak, and the living room displayed open glass picture windows, which provided a panoramic view of the surrounding fields and mountain tops. It had the feel of an intimate country club or a small tourist resort, with its intricately designed woodwork and homemade quilted tapestries and blankets throughout.

The girls explored the bathroom and kitchen while Tommy checked out the two small, but neatly kept bedrooms.

"We plan on living here and opening a summer getaway for disadvantaged adults and youth." Tara related to the Real-estate Agent and the older man. He was the caretaker of the property.

Tommy let them talk as he took a deeper look around, checking the water faucets and the bathrooms. He didn't see many electrical outlets and there were no cable or internet capabilities.

"It will take a lot to update the land and the cabins with accessible entrances and pathways." Tara related. "But this could be a perfect location for our business endeavor."

When it was time to leave, they said their goodbyes and they thanked their hosts for their time, as well as their kindness in showing them the property.

On the way back down the steps, Tara screamed out frightfully, thinking that she was almost going to fall.

Though, Tommy felt bad, and he hadn't let her fall, he was confused, by the way she hadn't let him carry her.

Instead, she had insisted on being carried awkwardly, while sitting down, along with the weight and the metal turning wheels of her chair.

However, it had been a good day, and they were all glad to have seen the property together.

In the early morning, Tommy would have to leave. The mechanic shop opened at eight, and he'd need to be there when they opened for repairs.

He would have to make excuses to leave, even though he wasn't really ready to go.

Hope wasn't ready for him to leave, either. She planned to slip into the bed beside him when the lights went out, if she could sneak under his covers quickly enough. The dogs often jumped at the slightest sound of movement in the dark, so she'd have to be quiet. And hopefully, he wouldn't turn her away.

She knew he was in-love with her mom, but she was on the pill, and she only wanted to have sex. She wanted to fuck him before he left. She would even let him hold his hand over her mouth, to muffle her excitement, if he wanted. She wouldn't mind.

Heather was ready for him to go. She liked him. He seemed to be a good guy. But she hadn't planned on him being there all weekend.

"His tire was flat? Big deal. Put on the spare. Call a frigging tow truck. Go home." She thought to herself.

She was very confused about her feelings for Tommy.

She felt guilty for having sex with him because she felt it was wrong. While at the same time, he had made her body feel pleasures she had never thought possible. He made her blush every time he caught her staring at him.

She had lost her virginity to him. And she had sucked him. But whether she liked it or not, he was still her mom's new boyfriend. While she had come to realize, she wasn't a lesbian, because of how he'd made her feel, she had also come to the realization that she was not like her sister, either. She wasn't a nymphomaniac. And she didn't want to be. But she was still confused. And she knew he remembered nothing.

"Mom and Hope have been vying for his attention all weekend." Heather thought to herself. "Don't they have any scruples? Don't they know what they were doing was wrong?" She continued to think. "They are both being very disrespectful of Dad, too. He is right upstairs. Don't they have any depth of feeling? And don't they know how I feel about him, too?"

Later that evening, while Hope and Heather sat in the living room watching movies, their mom sat with Tommy outside on the porch.

Tara placed her hand on Tommy's leg as the darkness of the waning hours fell upon them, near the windows, in the light. And she slowly moved her hand to his crotch.

She wasn't ready to watch him leave, as she smiled at him seductively, and as she slowly rubbed him through his jeans. She didn't think she would be able to make love to him, with her girls wide awake in the living room, and just the other side of the windows. But she really wanted to. And, she was seriously thinking about it, as she unzipped his zipper, and pulled him out.

"You're so hard." She said in a whisper excitedly.

Her heart began to beat fast.

Tommy was excited by the risk. It felt dangerous being exposed, where her two teenage daughters could see him the instant they walked outside. He didn't mean for it to happen, but he grew bigger at the thought.

"The girls might come out any minute." Tommy said to Tara as she began to stroke him.

"Shhhhhh," she sounded with her finger to his lips.

Tara enjoyed the risk as well. And she had not only seen his growth, but she had also felt him growing in her hands. She leaned over in her chair, and she kissed him.

"Stand up." She instructed.

Tommy stood up and did as he was told. And he met Hope's gaze through the picture glass window.

It was two-thirty-five in the morning. PJ drove his truck past her house, again. Tommy's car was still in the driveway.

"Mother-fucker!" He shouted out the window as he pounded his steering wheel and took off flying. "I fucking hate that son-of-a-bitch."

Michael, who had been inebriated all weekend, and who had also been asleep, for most of its entirety, stood in the doorway of their guest house, in the shadows, behind the light.

And he popped the top open on a can of old Yuengling Lager.

"Bitch," he said solemnly after he took a sip of cold beer.

And then he watched his wife, pleasuring another man.

Chapter Four – An Angelic Figure

He awakened with a fright at three-forty-two in the morning. He had barely fallen asleep just moments before. The room was dark as he lay upon Heather's bed. Bear and Susie had entered the room unexpectedly, and were excitedly prancing around, as their long nails and paws danced happily, and sharply upon its wooden floor.

As his vision came more into focus, he could see an angelic figure, quietly shushing them, and swiftly herding them from the room. Hope was barefoot, wearing a small white top that revealed her waist and her bellybutton, and a small pair of pink panties. As she turned to enter the doorway, Tommy realized he was mistaken. She was wearing a thong.

Hope reminded him so much of her mom when she was younger. Her legs were just as smooth and long and tanned. And the cheeks of her ass were equally and as excitingly succulent and inviting, as they jiggled when she walked across the room.

He couldn't help but notice. The moonlight had crossed through the bedroom window curtains at just the right angle, to reveal her.

She was right there in front of him. And it had all happened so fast.

He had been asleep, though, in his dreams, he could swear she had just crawled up under his covers, before

53

the dogs had come in, and had brushed the softness of her backside against him.

He recalled the moment at the party.

And he had the slowly fading memories of the dreams he'd had afterwards.

She was a very promiscuous young lady. And he was a grown man. But he was becoming very confused by the way he was reacting to the sights, the subtle stares and the seemingly innocent touches he was receiving.

Tommy got up out of bed and took a long, cold shower.

Tara and Heather were sleeping on the pull-out bed in the living room, when he made his way, stepping over them through the dark. He quietly left them sleeping and closed and locked the door behind him as he walked out through the back door onto the porch.

The air was cool and refreshing as he reached into his pocket for a cigarette and put it to his lips. He stood in the darkness upon their porch as he dialed triple A.

They would have their driver meet him at the end of Tara's graveled road, by seven-thirty in the morning. It was an hour and a half wait, but he didn't mind. He would sit on the swing for a few minutes, trying not to awaken anyone from sleep, and then he'd saunter down to his car and patiently wait inside, while he listened to the radio.

It had been an awesome weekend. A new tire was going to cost him a few bucks, but it had been more than worth the spending of a few dollars, to have been made a guest in Tara's home for the last two nights.

"Did we go on the charity walk this Saturday morning? Or was that last weekend?" Tommy couldn't recall. "Either way," he thought further. "We made the front page of the local paper."

He reflected on all they had done together over the past few days as he rounded the corner of the house by the two-car garage. It was still dark outside, except for the light of the moon, and a telephone pole light on either side of the property. But it was light enough for him to see that Michael's car was gone.

"He must have left sometime in the night." Tommy said to himself. He couldn't remember seeing him all weekend long. Since before they had driven four-wheelers down to the creek.

He knew Michael's car had been there when they had returned, because PJ had parked his truck beside it briefly, before Tara had sent him home.

"Seth had told me this was a hornet's nest." He told himself as he walked down the graveled road. "I just never realized how much I would enjoy being stung." He thought the analogy was funny.

Suddenly, two small shadows ran up beside him. He was startled at first. But then he realized it was Susie and Bear. He reached down and petted them as they excitedly accepted his touches. They seemed to have an endless supply of affection and saliva. He thought he had left them quietly inside when he, himself, had stepped out.

"Someone must have gotten up and let them out." He thought as he turned around suddenly and saw the small light that had been turned on by a window.

Tommy said goodbye to Bear and Susie, and he left them standing outside his car, and he closed the door.

"You are listening to channel 106.9 WFKM FM." The radio said. "Stay tuned for another classic block of classic rock, right here on your classic rock station. 106.9 WFKM. It's seven-thirty-two in the blessed A.M. and we're playing the music you love. Music …that Rocks you Like a Hurricane."

As the music of The Scorpions filled the car, the beat resonated and vibrated off the windows glass. Just as the approaching vehicle, that was slowly being driven down the roadway, signaled its turn into the driveway, with blinking yellow lights. Tommy got out and stood beside his car.

"Do you have a flat tire?" The driver asked.

Tommy wanted to reply with, "No. That would be politically incorrect. I don't have a flat tire. My tire is directionally challenged. Here's your sign."

But he didn't say it out loud. It was too early in the morning and this guy just might actually, be, a Redneck.

But he thought it was funny in his mind. And Bill Engvall would've been proud.

"I don't have a spare, but I could use a lift to the service station in town." Tommy answered.

"No problem, my name is Jim." The driver said. "Aren't you Lynn's brother."

"Yes," he replied. "I'm Tommy. How do you know my sister?"

"We went out a couple of times back in high school." Jim replied. "I haven't thought about her in years."

Tommy was too tired to pay much attention to the ramblings of a Tow Truck operator at seven-forty-five in the morning, after being awake almost all night. He sat in the passenger seat as the truck rolled down the winding road and onto the main highway.

The sunlight soon came over the horizon in bright red and orange colors. Tommy slipped on his sunglasses and stared out at the skies.

He had taken the day off from work, because of his car tire.

And he looked forward to having it fixed quickly, so he could make his way home and fall into bed. It was eight-fourteen in the morning when they pulled into the service station, and Tommy walked inside.

"Having some trouble with your tire I see." The service attendant said as he greeted him with a handshake.

"Yes sir." Tommy answered. "I'm not sure how it happened. I must have driven over something Saturday morning and I've just let it sit."

"We'll get it checked out for you, no problem." The attendant replied.

Tommy walked outside into the parking lot, hearing the jingling of the bells on the front door as it opened, and he watched his car being unloaded and the driver waving goodbye, as he pulled away.

"I'm damn glad I took the day off." He thought as he looked at his watch and lit up another cigarette.

The air was heating up quickly, as the sun rose higher in the sky. It was already stuffy out. His forehead was beginning to form perspiration beneath his dirty bandanna.

"Ding. Ring. Ring," Tommy's phone rang out. It was Tiffany. She was a girl he hadn't heard from in a very long time.

"Hello stranger," her familiar voice called out. "How've you been?"

Tiffany was a sweet and caring young soul. She was twenty-three years old.

Tommy had met her at a social function a couple of years ago, and she had taken to him instantly. She had lived a rough life. Her mother had died when she was nine years old, from an infectious disease known as meningitis. And even more unfortunately, her mother's death had left her in the care of an abusive stepfather.

After her mother's death, Meghan contracted a rare form of sensorineural hearing loss. It had left her almost completely deaf.

Through everything, however, she had remained strong. She was a fighter. And she always held herself to a positive outlook.

"I'm doing well." Tommy answered. "How have you been?"
"I've been doing great." She answered. "I've got something to tell ya."

Tiffany looked to Tommy as a positive role model in her life, a father figure. He had been there for her through some difficult times in her life, and he meant the world to her.

"I'm having a party next month." She said. "So, I'm giving you plenty of notice. I want you to meet my fiancé."

"Congratulations." Tommy said excitedly. "I'm so happy for you. Tell him I'm bringing my pistol and shotgun, so he'd better treat you right."

"You're so funny." Tiffany laughed. "By the way, Meghan will be there, too. I hope that's okay?"

Tommy paused.

Meghan was a twenty-something, smoking hot and extremely promiscuous woman, who had attempted to dig her claws into Tommy's ass many times.

She was aggressive and tenacious when they had been together. And after their break-up, she had continued her obsessive behaviors, and had even intervened a time or two, in another of Tommy's relationships. So, he was rightfully a little hesitant and gun-shy whenever her name was mentioned. But he was grateful for the warning.

"I've told her that I was inviting you, and for her to behave herself." Tiffany emphasized. "If she doesn't, I'll make her leave. Tommy, I swear."

"It'll be fine." Tommy answered. "I can handle the amorous affections of a crazy woman for one night."

"See you then. Seven-thirty. Don't be late." Tiffany continued. "I can't wait for you to meet Mark." She said as she hung up the phone.

Tommy placed his phone in his back pocket, just as the service center attendant opened the door and asked him to step inside.

"Did you get it fixed, or do I need a brand-new tire?" Tommy asked.

"I've got something to show you." The attendant said as he led him through the service bay doors to his vehicle.

Tommy's tire was still flat as he pointed out a red circle that had been drawn and outlined to show where the tire had been punctured.

"You see this perforation." He declared. "It's on the sidewall. You didn't run over anything. It's a thin and even slice. It's been pierced."

Tommy looked back at the service attendant.

"Have you pissed anyone off?" He chuckled unintentionally, "Because, your tire's been stabbed with a knife."

Tommy cocked his head to one side and wondered.

"Are you sure it was cut with a knife blade?" Tommy asked.

"Yes sir," The attendant answered. "It's on the outer sidewall, and the puncture is thin and flat. It's a pocket-knife size cut."

Tommy touched it with his fingers.

"We don't carry that size tire in stock." The attendant continued as they walked back inside. "We'll have to order a new one. But it'll be here tomorrow morning. We can have it done first thing."

"Order two of them." Tommy replied. "If someone's trying to scare me off, it may be good to have a spare."

Tommy left his key at the front service desk, and he pulled out a cigarette and lit it with a flame. And then he called and took a taxi ride home.

TONY NALLEY

THE DARKNESS IN THE SHADOWS

Chapter Five – Lights from the Fire

It was still early morning as he sat in his fading-white colored wicker chair, on the back deck, overlooking his back yard. The shadow covered lawn was outlined on one side by towering blue spruce trees, and tall oaks and pines on the other that stood along the fence row before him.

Tommy lived in a nice, quiet, upper-middle class neighborhood, in a three bedroom, two bath-room home.

The two-toned brick house had a large attached two-car garage that opened up into a fully finished basement. It also had nice hardwood floors that encompassed the whole of the upper living quarters, the hallways and the adjoining staircase.

He often sat in the swing, beneath the shade of his umbrella tree in the back, as he played guitar and enjoyed his late evenings. Though in the mornings, he found refuge from the rising sun on his back deck, beside the coolness of the brick accompanied by the sounds of rippling water from his outdoor Jacuzzi.

Tommy knew he needed to tell her. Someone had elevated their dissatisfaction to his presence and to the blossoming relationship between himself and Tara. It was an open threat. This action not only had been done physically, but also; it had been done with malice aforethought. It was a criminal action, with psychological implications.

There were two logical suspects. PJ, the hot-headed ex-boyfriend with an inferiority complex, coupled with his stalker, and physically violent personality. And Michael, the little boy who lived upstairs; he was shut off and starving for affection and for his parental rights, who also was drowning his anger and frustrations in thousands of dollars' worth of alcoholic poisons.

Either way Tommy broached this issue, he knew Tara would be defensive of her household, as a lioness to her cubs. But she had to know, and he would have to tell her. So, he picked up his phone and he dialed her number.

"Hey beautiful, good morning," he said as they exchanged the normal pleasantries. "I got my car towed. Apparently, it's a special-order tire, so I bought a second one for a spare. It'll be delivered tomorrow and fixed by early morning so that's two days off for me." He continued. "Completely circumstantial but, there was a half inch straight cut in the sidewall of the tire."

"I am so sorry." Tara answered. "I want to know how this happened. Did they indicate if it was a slow leak? Was the object still in the tire? Was it in the sidewall? I'm really bothered by this. I'm so sorry. And you really should have woken me up. At least I could have waited with you and driven you home."

"You are sweet. It wasn't something I ran over, Babe." Tommy said. "It was deliberate. It was a knife blade. The tire guy agreed. I'm keeping the old tire to show you. It's not your fault. And when I left this morning, Bear and Susie stayed with me the whole time."

"Oh, my gosh. Are you serious?" Tara said. "I'm just really pissed. I have ZERO time nor tolerance for this shit. I WILL figure this out. We have to have something on video."

"Don't get yourself upset." Tommy said calmly. "Things happen in life. I can handle myself well. You just enjoy your day and have fun with the girls."

"No, threats are a new ballgame." She answered. "Not to be taken lightly. I've lived here for years, and I've felt one-hundred percent safe; for someone to know my situation and then, on top of that, do something like this? No."

"Quick question, and please, for the love of God, be honest with me." Tara continued. "Do you know anything more about this PJ thing than I know?"

"I don't know anything more than what you've told me and what I've seen when he's been around. Why?" Tommy asked.

"Because he's just being 'pissy' and just saying things to mess with my head and I don't need this. I just would love to have one friend who is being straight with me." Tara related. "And now, with the tire incident on top of his recent calls and texts, the girls are going to be scared to death. Heather is NOT going to be sleeping in her room again and I am monumentally pissed off. I'm sorry," she continued. "I'm not mad at you. I'm just venting, I guess." Tara paused. "Tommy, I've got to get the girls up and get some school shopping done today. I'll call you later tonight if that's okay?"

"Sure," Tommy answered. "I'll speak with you then."

As the call ended, Tommy went inside and put on a pot of coffee and grabbed a strawberry pop-tart. It tasted wonderful. He hadn't realized how hungry he had become.

As he poured a cup of hot brew into his mug, and stirred in the vanilla cream and sugar, his thoughts ran rampant.

PJ was the obvious choice. He had invaded his territory, and he was more like an angry dog pissing on every tree.

But Michael had a huge investment in time, money and family to lose. He didn't know Tara had already been planning to divorce him, and Tommy's presence was a thorn in his side.

"It was definitely a hornet's nest." He mumbled to himself as he stepped back outside and sat down again in his chair.

Tommy sipped his coffee and stared out across the blue-clear skies.

Suddenly, something he had read on Facebook a few days back crossed his mind. It was funny and quite amusing; however, as much as he would like to dismiss its validity entirely, there had been some sound and reasonable assertions to its claims.

It was called the Hot Crazy Matrix.

Hotness:
Do not waste time with girls who fall between a five and a seven on the hotness axis. It will screw up your frame of mind and make you do things you normally wouldn't do. The hotness level also needs to be realistic in comparison to what you physically look like. You need to always be maximizing your appearance and physique because you can't expect to attract hot girls if you are not up to par yourself. Hotness is determined immediately upon meeting a new girl. A nice body is arbitrary, as people prefer different body types, heights, etc.

Crazy:
All girls start with a default level of a four for craziness. If the girl is in the seven to ten hotness ranges, it is inevitable that the girl is going to be completely bat-shit-crazy, at the very least an eight to ten crazy. She's most likely a dancer, a stripper, etc. This level of hotness and crazy can be dangerous. You may find yourself getting into fights, having your property stolen, and you may also have your tires slashed.

Tommy paused and thought about that. Tara was definitely in the eight- point-five to ten on the hotness range. Her level of crazy however, was still in question.

The 'wife zone' is a girl who is an eight to ten hot, and only a five to seven crazy.

It can take weeks, often months, to determine the true nature of a girl.

Women are naturally deceptive and elusive with their true persona, so it may take a long time to figure out what you have. More often than not, you have to determine what level of crazy you can put up with for the long-term, if you are considering a relationship.

Anything between an eight to ten hot, and between a one to three crazy, is a potential tranny, so you need to be careful.

Unicorn:
A unicorn is any girl between an eight to ten hot and 'only' a one or lower crazy. If you find one of these, you should be very careful and try not to spook her. She will spook very easily. Call a medical professional to help you evaluate her hotness versus her craziness more effectively, because these girls don't actually exist. You are having a hallucination or a witch's spell has been cast upon you. Because, based upon all recorded analysis, this girl does not exist, she is a Unicorn.

Once you realize that men and women have massive fundamental differences in their ways of thinking; you will have a better understanding on how to deal with their personalities. There are definitely many crazy, broken girls out there with horrible views on how society should work.

Tommy finished his coffee and grabbed another pop-tart on the way to his bedroom. It had been a full weekend. And he was tired. He hit the bed face first with a bounce and closed his eyes. As he slept, he began to dream. But it wasn't an ordinary kind of dreaming.

The dreams seemed real and interconnected. He could smell the scents of the woods and he could feel the grass.

He could interact with a host of others who communicated with him. It was eerie, and it was in full, intense and vivid color.

In his dreams, he owned a rickety old bluish grey house in the middle of a park-like wood. There were faces he knew, distantly familiar faces and people who were walking upon his lawn, and there were still others who acted as though he knew them.

A young girl, of about twelve or thirteen years of age, got out of an old, red nineteen-fifty style Chevrolet Fleetline automobile, near a broken wooden fence, and walked through the grass to speak with him. The car she had gotten out of was brightly painted, as though it were brand new or as if it had been kept in a covered garage. It was in pristine condition, highlighted by new white-wall tires, stainless steel and shiny chrome. The girl was blonde, and she was dressed in a pastel blue sweater and matching shorts. She wore catholic schoolgirl shoes of brown and white.

"I'm looking to earn some money." The girl said. "I'm good at babysitting and I can cook and clean."

"I don't have any children." Tommy told her. "Is that your family in the car?"

"Yes." She stated. "We've been evicted from our home and we're looking for work."

In his dream, he didn't recall inviting her inside. But the next thing he knew, she was in his kitchen, and he was sitting in his small living room with her family. They were hillbilly country, except for the girl's father, who was dressed in Civil War Military Dress. Nonetheless, they appeared gruff and unclean, and he could smell something old and sour. They had brought a large wooden funeral casket with them. It sat in the center of the room, as everyone sat around it. It was really strange and weird. He thought someone was inside it.

Suddenly, Tommy became aware that his mom was standing behind him, and she whispered in his ear.

"Don't feed them." She warned. "They will never leave."

Then, the young girl came out of his kitchen carrying a large platter filled with food. He noticed it was mostly piled with meats, there were hams and sausages and pepperonis.

At that moment, his dream became a nightmare.

The girl and her family changed into ravenous beasts and hungrily growled and gnashed their teeth as they devoured the food. Blood splattered from the food tray and was splashed all over the walls as they clawed at it.

More blood poured out from beneath the coffin's lid and began to flood over its sides and cover the floor.

He saw witches clawing. He saw wolf-like beasts.

He heard their cackling and laughter.

He heard the howling roars.

He saw blood streaming down the walls.

And then Tommy woke the hell up.

"Welcome back ladies and gentlemen. It's one twenty-seven A.M. You are listening to 107.4 AM WMKB Macabre Radio, as we rejoin our scheduled program already in progress."

"The person you think of as "yourself" only exists in your mind. Every person you meet, every person you have a relationship with or even anyone you make eye contact with, or meet on the street, creates a different version of you within their mind." The person on the radio said. "You are not the same person to your mom, your dad, your sisters and brothers that you are to your neighbors, your co-workers or to your friends. There are thousands of different versions of you out there, in other people's minds. A "you" exists in each version, and yet your 'you', yourself, isn't really someone at all. Your 'you', only exists in your mind."

Tommy turned off the radio.

"I don't need that shit in my fucking head at one-thirty in the morning." He said out loud to himself. "Damn. Dreams about witches and awful werewolf looking beasts. Fucking coffins and blood. Fuck. I've got to get up."

Tommy got out of bed and took a quick warm shower, and then he dressed for a road trip. He needed to drive.

For some reason, he felt he needed to be somewhere, nowhere, but anywhere but here.

Twenty minutes later, he found himself driving down a one-lane winding road, outlined on either side by thick wood and tall grass, and he drove cautiously.

"I'm not stalking her." He said to himself. "I just happen to be driving down her road."

Tara was becoming a focal point in his life, and he felt a very strong inclination to be near her. He crossed the flowing creek, by way of a low-lying cream-colored concrete bridge, and noticed a glowing fire through the darkness. It was further down the creek bed, than he had been with Tara and her girls, so, he decided to follow the road slowly to get a better glimpse of the fire.

As he passed Tara's house, PJ's white truck stood out to him like a slap in his face. It was parked in her driveway, and none of the lights were on inside her house. Tommy didn't come here to spy on her, but after seeing the truck, he felt suspiciously guilty.

"Son-of-a-bitch." He thought to himself.

He continued following the light from the fire as he passed her house, and he remained driving along the one-lane road around the bend. He drove slowly, all the while, making sure his headlights were low and not shining directly through the woods. As his car began to line up parallel to the light, he pulled off the road and into the grass, and he quickly turned off the car's headlights.

Tommy breathed in deeply, and he grabbed his nine-millimeter pistol from the car console. He checked it. It was loaded. He clicked the safety off and he stepped out into the dark.

As he tread through the tall grass and weeds, he found a stopping place between the fire and the shelter of the woods, and he leaned against an old tree to get a better view of the flame. The lights from the fire flickered brightly through the shadows and danced upon the bark of the old tree.

Tommy turned and looked up.

The tree he was leaning against resembled the head of a very large donkey.

His hand was resting upon its long equine nose.

AND THIS MOTHER-FUCKER HAD EYES.

It took a quick minute for him to calm himself down.

His heart raced and beat heavily within his chest.

He didn't think he had made too much noise. Though he realized he would have spooked any deer that may have been around. Slowly and stealthily, he moved closer to the firelight, brandishing his weapon, while keeping himself completely covered by the weeds and brush that had grown thick between the trees. And then he saw them.

There were seven, maybe eight people, no wait; there were twelve people standing around the fire. They were singing, maybe, or chanting something. They all wore black robes with hoods.

Tommy remembered his grandpa's voice and the words he spoke to him one night, while he told him of something he had seen, along a darkened one-lane road.

"I can't say as I was ever scared of nothing." He remembered him saying. "But I knew right then that there was someplace else that I needed to be."

Tommy hastily made his way back to his car and started the engine. He found a turnaround spot and quickly drove back past the Donkey tree and the fire and turned abruptly into Tara's driveway. He didn't care that PJ was there. If she was going to see him behind his back, so what, life would go on.

He raced out of his car, noticing both their cars were in the driveway, and he ran up to the back door and began pounding it hard with his fists.

"Tara." He shouted. "Tara, somebody open up. It's me, it's Tommy."

No one answered. There was no movement inside the house, no lights, and no sounds. Susie and Bear weren't even barking. They weren't inside, and he saw no sign of them anywhere in the dark.

"Damn it." He shouted.

Tommy quickly climbed back into his car and pulled out his cell phone.

"Hey girl, how are you?" He texted quickly, "I know it's late, but I also know you're a night owl."

Almost immediately, Tara replied.

"Me and the girls are staying at mom's tonight," she texted. "Hope you're having a great night."

"She's staying with her mom?" Tommy thought. "Interesting, her car is here, and PJ's truck is here, very interesting."

"Have fun," Tommy texted in reply.

"What the fuck is going on here?" He said out loud to hear himself think. "I need to get the fuck out of here, go somewhere safe, get something to eat and I need to call Seth." He breathed deeply. "Fuck. What have I gotten myself into?"

As he made his way back over the creek, and across the cream-colored concrete bridge, he noticed the glowing fires still burning through the gloom. He stopped long enough to light a cigarette, lock his doors, and then he drove like a bat-out-of-hell out of there.

And the music played loudly over his stereo speakers.

♫ There goes my old girlfriend, there's another diamond ring And, uh, all those late-night promises, I guess they don't mean a thing. So baby, what's the story? Did you find another man? Is it easy to sleep in the bed that we made? When you don't look back I guess the feelings start to fade away. I used to feel your fire but now it's cold inside. And you're back on the street like you didn't miss a beat, yeah, tell me what it takes to let you go. Tell me how the pain's supposed to go. Tell me how it is that you can sleep, in the night. Without thinking you lost everything that was good in your life to the toss of the dice. Tell me what it takes to let you go, yeah. ♫

♫ Girl, before I met you I was F.I.N.E. Fine. But your love made me a prisoner, yeah my heart's been doing time. You spent me up like money then you hung me out to dry. It was easy to keep all your lies in disguise.

Cause you had me in deep with the devil in your eyes. Tell me what it takes to let you go. Tell me how the pain's supposed to go. Tell me how it is that you can sleep, in the night, without thinking you lost everything that was good in your life to the toss of the dice? Tell me what it takes to let you go. ♫ Aerosmith

Chapter Six – Sacred Blessing Ceremony

By a candle's light, in the dark of the night, she placed the herbs of sage and sweet grass, which were twisted into a braided strand, into her medicine smudge bowl and she lit the flame. The wooden bowl represented water, the waters of life. The herbs and its ashes represented mother earth. She directed the smoke from the fire, representing the air, with an eagle's feather, a gift from her winged friend. And she brought the smoke into her, in swirls over her head, shoulders and around her body.

She paid attention to the cardinal directions of east, west, and north, south and above and below. And she called out to her spirit guides in her native tongue.

Raven was Native American, a direct descendant of Chief Joseph of the Cherokee Nation. She was beautiful; she was intelligent, harmonious and funny. And she was one of Tommy's dearest and most trusted friends. He was part of her Heart Circle, and from one-hundred-fifty miles away, she felt he was in danger.

The smoke poured out heavily from the fire within the bowl. As her chanting reached crescendo, her room, with opened windows, was shrouded and enveloped with thick black undulating clouds of smoke.

The fires raged. It wasn't expected. And the fire grew larger.

"Oh my," Raven exclaimed. "This is serious."

At two-twenty-three in the morning, Raven called her mentors, her elders, and her mother teachers of the spiritual covenants. And by two-thirty-four in the morning, there were now, four medicine bowls smoking, and four Native American Medicine Women, from the Shawnee, Eskimo and Cherokee and Sioux Nations, participating in the Sacred Smoke Bowl Blessing Ceremony.

Seth worked the night shift at the hospital in West Virginia. If he weren't working, Tommy knew he would still be awake. It was difficult for him, always switching from third shift to first shift daylight hours. Tommy never knew whether or not he would be sleeping, at work or wide awake and binge-watching Netflix.

He dialed his number while driving.

"What the fuck, man?" Seth exclaimed. "What are you doing up at two-thirty in the morning, everything alright?"

"It's a hornet's nest, brother." Tommy answered. "I should have listened. You won't believe the kind of shit I've just witnessed."

Tommy related the story, all the while he admitted it sounded crazy and that he must have suddenly lost his mind. He pulled his car into a Walmart parking lot beneath a tree in the back, just out of the blinding lights, and he lit up a cigarette. It was easier to talk sitting still, than while driving.

"Fire, brother, fires in the woods with people dressed in black robes." He related. "Some scary occultist shit man. Chanting and singing and a big ass Donkey tree thing in the fucking woods."

"What the fuck, brother?" Seth replied. "Oh my God, she's a fucking witch."

"I told you she was a witch." A voice came from the background. Seth had Tommy on the speaker phone. "Tell Thomas …tell him I told you that she was a witch." Seth's wife stated.

"Sienna says to tell you that Tara's a witch." Seth related. "Though, I'm sure you probably heard that."

"I don't know if she was one of them." Tommy said. "I didn't see any faces. I was just out driving because I couldn't sleep. Her car was in the driveway, but all her lights were out. And when I knocked on the door, there was no one home, not even her dogs were barking. I texted her, and she said they were staying the night at her mom's."

Seth continued to listen while Tommy formulated his next words.

"I haven't even told you about my tire." Tommy continued. "Someone put a knife in my tire the other night while it was parked in her driveway."

"You've been threatened." Seth stated. "You were getting too close, and someone wanted you out of the picture." Seth continued while slightly laughing. "No amount of pussy is worth that man, I don't care how good it was, or how good it is. You need to back away and completely remove yourself from the situation."

"It was definitely a threat." Tommy answered. "Her husband was at home the entire day, and PJ not only knew we were at the creek but called her while we were sitting there by the fire. And I could swear that I saw his truck cross over the little bridge on his way to her house, just minutes afterward."

"Listen brother, we've already discussed the amount of traumatic abuse this woman endured in her childhood. And we've also discussed the psychological implications that commonly arise when these abusive situations occur." Seth related. "Taking everything into consideration, along with the obvious occultist ceremony you've just been made witness to; you've got to remove yourself from the situation. You've got to get the fuck out."

"She's a witch, Thomas!" Sienna shouted from the background.

"I'd better let you guys go." Tommy stated. "I've got to clear my mind and get some sleep."

"Be careful, brother." Seth said. "Watch after yourself."

Tommy got out of his car and walked across the parking lot. The store was open twenty-four seven, and he needed to stretch his legs and think. He picked up a few CD's: Willie Nelson, Counting Crows, the last album released by Johnny Cash and a CD by Journey that was overflowing with classic love ballads. His taste in music was diversified. He felt the need to stimulate different sides of his brain.

He returned to his car with a sack filled with snacks and soda about forty-five minutes later. And he fell asleep in the parking lot beneath the tree and the dancing shadows of lamppost lights, almost an hour after that. He alternated CDs in his stereo player, whenever he was awakened by the sounds of cars passing by, or the lights from their headlights. By eleven-twenty in the morning, the heat from the sun awakened him fully.

He slipped on his aviator sunglasses and started his car.

The air conditioning cooled him down quickly as he made his way home, where he proceeded to take a long cold shower.

Tommy began to rationalize everything he had seen, heard and felt. One of the functions of the human brain is to maintain normalcy. Maybe he had only perceived a normal common occurrence, a cookout in the woods.

And perhaps it was only a coincidence that Tara and her girls had just so happened to be visiting with her mom and their grandma overnight. He couldn't find reason for PJ's truck being parked alongside hers in her driveway, nor could he understand why hers was parked their as well. He couldn't ask her. He would seem as creepy as PJ.

"Maybe, she likes that," he thought. "She seems to surround herself with men who have violent and irrational tendencies."

Tommy had heard Tara say, on multiple occasions, that PJ was a good man.

He had also heard her say that her husband, Michael, was a good man.

PJ was a hot-headed asshole, who stalked her and was physically assertive; some might say he was violent, while Michael was a verbally and physically abusive alcoholic.

At the moment, it was the first time he was ever glad to have NOT been categorized by her, as a good man. He didn't know the criteria by which they were being judged. He didn't like the company he would be in. And he didn't want to be included in such a disreputable group of men.

Suddenly, as he got out of the shower, Tommy's phone rang.

"Tommy, we need to talk." Raven said.

"Sure," Tommy answered. "What's up?"

"Before you say anything, I need to tell you about a dream I had." Raven said. "I had a dream about this young blond girl. She rang my doorbell, and I answered the door. I could see her mom waiting in the car outside with the motor running."

Tommy began to relate Raven's dream of a young blonde girl, to the one who had invaded his dreams the night before.

"The car was red." Raven continued. "It was some sort of older car from the late fifties or early nineteen-sixties. Anyway, the girl needed a place to stay and for some reason I let her in. She slept in the living room, and I felt in the dream as though I was a mother figure. As the dream continued the girl began to steal from me and began to control events in my life. Needless to say, I kicked her out of my house." Raven continued. "The following day, in my dream, the doorbell rang again. This time when I opened the door the girl and her mother stood together on my front porch. They both wanted in. I picked up my double-barrel shotgun and shouted at them to leave."

Raven paused for a moment.

87

"I know it's weird, but it scared the hell out of me, Tommy." She related. "As they drove away, I saw your face in the backseat of their car. You were staring at me, through the back driver side window."

As Raven talked, Tommy stepped outside and lit up a cigarette. When she had finished talking, he proceeded to relate the story of the dream he'd had the previous night. And he highlighted the correlations of his to hers.

"Wow." Raven shouted. "Wow. I knew it. I knew it. I knew it meant something."

"What does it mean?" Tommy asked.

"You're seeing someone aren't you?" Raven answered. "You love this girl. I mean, you really LOVE this girl, don't you?" She didn't pause long enough for him to answer. "There is a dark aura that is surrounding you my dear friend. You are in immediate and life-threatening danger."

Tommy related some of his experiences over the past few weeks; he spoke of his sliced tire, his wildly erotic dreams, and the hooded people who were chanting around the fire.

Raven informed him of her medicinal roles within her tribe. And she told him of her smudge bowl.

"The smoke was black, Tommy." She stated. "It was blacker and thicker than anything I've ever seen. It filled my entire house, and all the windows were completely open. And the fire was high. Higher and hotter than hellfire. It burned my two-hundred-year-old bowl. My mentor was concerned as well. She joined me in the blessing ritual. Her house was filled with black smoke as well."

"I believe you." Tommy answered. "There have been some incredible warning signs the entire time we've been together." Tommy paused. "I guess she's not the same girl I once knew and loved. Perhaps, that girl no longer exists."

"She has got such a hold on you." Raven stated. "You need to take those rose-colored glasses off and take a good long look at the situation. She's a witch, Tommy. She has definitely placed a spell on you." Raven continued. "My bowl is two-hundred-years-old, Tommy. It's never caught on fire. Never. I'll need to bury it in the earth for thirty days to release the negative energy and replenish the goodness from mother earth."

Tommy sat quietly and listened.

"Her girls are in this too. You know that, right? It was one of her girls, if not both, who invaded our dreams." Raven continued. "Ultimately, you will have to make a decision. And when you do, own it, believe it and act upon it."

"Thank you Raven for caring about me." Tommy answered. "I'm proud to be a part of your heart-circle."

As they spoke, music played upon Tommy's stereo.

♫ Childhood living is easy to do. The things you wanted I bought them for you. Graceless lady you know who I am. You know I can't let you slide through my hands. Wild horses couldn't drag me away. Wild, wild horses couldn't drag me away. ♫

♫ I watched you suffer a dull aching pain. Now you've decided to show me the same. No sweeping exit or offstage lines. Could make me feel bitter or treat you unkind. Wild horses couldn't drag me away. Wild, wild horses couldn't drag me away. I know I've dreamed you a sin and a lie. I have my freedom, but I don't have much time. Faith has been broken tears must be cried. Let's do some living after we die. Wild horses couldn't drag me away. Wild, wild horses we'll ride them someday. Wild horses couldn't drag me away. Wild, wild horses we'll ride them someday. ♫ The Rolling Stones.

"You always will be." Raven answered as they said their goodbyes and hung up the phone. She would now have to bury her bowl in the soil for thirty days to release the negative energy and replenish the positive from the earth.

Tommy ordered a pizza and turned on his TV. It was an older model projection television, but it was new enough to have high definition and the picture was great. When his food arrived, he tipped the driver well and sat back on his couch in the living room and devoured the slices. He was hungry. The past events weighed heavily on him and had taken a great deal of his strength.

90

"Hey stranger," Tara texted as his phones light lit up. "I haven't heard from you. I hope you're okay."

"I'm doing alright." Tommy stated. "Let's get together tonight."

"I'm sorry, I can't tonight." Tara stated. "Michael came home from his work trip without his car. He had a taxi drive him home from the airport. And he won't tell me why or where the car is."

"I understand." Tommy answered.

"We spent most of today at the hospital." She continued.

"Because when he came home, he was heavily intoxicated and became utterly belligerent. He was yelling and screaming and then he tripped and fell down the stairs. We thought he was dead." Tara exclaimed. "We called an ambulance, and they ran tests for hours. They released him a couple of hours ago, and we brought him back home. But I believe they should have kept him, due to his heart palpitations."

"I understand." Tommy answered again.

"Really, Tommy," Tara stated. "I'm sorry. Maybe we can get together again next weekend. We really need to move ahead with this business. I've done a lot of thinking about it and I'm ready to move forward."

"Sounds good," Tommy replied. "I'll talk with you again later in the week."

It was very hard for Tommy to keep his distance from Tara, even when it was through his use of cold words over the phone.

"By the way," Tara said. "PJ didn't knife your tire. He couldn't have. He tells me everything. He wouldn't be able to hold on to something like that. He couldn't keep it in. He just doesn't have the ability. Besides, it would be the stupidest plan to get rid of you ever. You spent the night at my house. How could he be stupid enough to do that if he wanted you gone?"

"Tara," Tommy replied. "I'm the victim here. It would be nice if you weren't the defense lawyer for everyone who had motive and you were actually on my side."

"I'm not taking sides." She replied defensively. "We have video cameras and I have reviewed them. Plus, I've reviewed neighbors' cameras as well. The only person that is seen going near that side of your car, Tommy, is you."

"Are you saying that I stabbed my own tire?" Tommy asked. "Please show me the videos. If I did it myself, then I need psychiatric help. Are you saying it's easier for you to believe that I'm a nut job, than to believe your Neanderthal boyfriend has an inferiority complex and acted out in anger like a jealous dumb ass?" Tommy continued. "Wow."

"You know," She replied. "PJ has never once said anything bad about you or called you any names."
"I'll bet he hasn't been banished to a three by five text window either, has he?" Tommy asked. "And he's just your friend, right?"

For the next few weeks Tara canceled every date they had scheduled. Once, she left him sitting in a parking lot for hours in his car, while she waited for her hair to be done at her beauty salon. That turned into a bad hair day for her, and she broke the date. So, Tommy took himself to a movie. And for the record, the movie sucked.

Another time, when he called to come over for a visit, he was turned away because she and her family were all outside mowing grass and weed eating the lawn.

Tara cried over the phone that day because it was the first time in years that her family had all pulled together to help her in the yard. One of her friends had stopped by to help her as well. She told Tommy of how happy it made her feel, to be a part of a real family moment again.

It went without saying. Tommy knew the friend she had mentioned was PJ.

She would continually text him however, at all hours of the night. She spoke of how she thought she was crazy, and she texted of this darkness she had inside of her. She wanted to change; she said she really wanted to. But she didn't know if she could. Tommy could have written a book with all of the words and stories she texted him.

She spoke of the monster inside of her, of how she never slept and of how no one had ever understood her like he did.

She continually told Tommy how much he meant to her and how important he was in her life.

Days and days had passed since he'd seen her. Even though they spoke through text every night, she continually made excuses for not having time to be together, while Tommy continued his life as though she were still in it.

He'd even made a few stops at the Dollar Tree to pick up prize gifts for their next Trivia contest. And he had bought a full-size functional skeleton for seven-dollars and ninety-five-cents at the Peddlers mall, to match the one Hope had in her room. But until he'd given it to her, he sat it up in the passenger seat of his car and placed a pair of sunglasses on it, and an old dirty bandanna upon its head for realism.

Tommy kept the faith, remembering the girl he once knew. And he often recalled the beautiful person she once had been. She was the one who had kissed him ever so sweetly, beneath the lights of a Christmas tree.

He had made a mistake then.

He hadn't fought for her.

And he had kept a promise to her, which he never should have made.

He had lost her forever because of that promise; a promise made when they were both only fourteen years old.

He loved her then.

He loved her now.

And he would love her, all of his life.

THE DARKNESS IN THE SHADOWS

Chapter Seven – The Great American Eclipse

The corporate office was unlike any other. The classically designed architecture was highlighted by neatly trimmed landscape, including green grass and bushes. It was aligned with large pine and oak trees, covering the brown pinecones and needles that lay beneath them. The foyer's interior was garnished with live and beautiful greenery and flowers, and it was brandished by squared marble floors. The vast open space spread upwards above the columns of stone, into large grandiose skylights, a full four floors directly up and unto the vaulted ceiling.

Tommy's corner office had large bay windows that overlooked the view of a lengthy man-made creek bed, with a picturesque walking bridge that traversed it.

During the rains, the waters flowed like rivers. But during the dry seasons, you could walk along its concrete base.

He was in the middle of a business meeting when she texted him. He had just scored a deal with Hampton Foods. The contract was signed, and the agreement closed, and it pocketed him a commissions' check of over six-thousand-dollars.

"I want you to come and see the eclipse with me," Tara texted. "The climax is at two-thirty this afternoon. Come and watch it with me?"

It was a once in a lifetime event. While total solar eclipses are not rare, they occur twice every three years on average and can be seen from some part of the Earth, a total eclipse of the Sun that can be seen from the American East Coast occurs less frequently. The last time an Eclipse was visible from coast to coast was almost one-hundred-years earlier, on June eighth, nineteen-eighteen.

What made the eclipse of August twenty-first, twenty-seventeen extra special, was that it would be the first time since the total solar eclipse of January eleventh, eighteen-eighty, that a total solar eclipse would occur exclusively over the continental United States. This is why the eclipse would later become known as the Great American Eclipse.

"Okay." Tommy agreed. "I just closed a large deal, and I'm sure I can walk out of here with no questions asked."

"Great." She replied. "I'll see you in a little while. We have some sunglasses for viewing it. And you can share mine."

Tommy left the building at ten-fifteen in the morning and began the hour and a half drive to Tara's house. Traffic was thick along thirty-one East, especially after he'd passed Mt. Washington, where a new bypass was being constructed. The road crew had closed the highway while they moved their heavy equipment over the older thoroughfare. And he sat completely still for over twenty minutes before he decided that he'd better call.

"I don't think I'm going to be able to make it." He said. "Traffic is at a halt. It's at a complete standstill."

"You still have time." Tara answered. "It's only eleven-forty. What are you going to do? Are you going to watch it from the road?"

"Okay," He answered. "I'll try."

Tommy hung up the phone and sat in the line of traffic. He turned on his radio to kill some time.

"You are listening to 107.4 AM WMKB Macabre Radio." The announcer said. "It's the dawning of a New Age, an age of magic. During the lunar eclipse occurring all across the United States, a witch will face his/her insecurity, you must not only be able to imagine that a change can occur and what the change will bring you, but you must also have the willpower to proclaim: I will make this happen. A lunar eclipse is the perfect time to face the past and find out the roots of your fears and insecurities. You are advised to seek guidance from your allies: angels, fairies, ghosts of loved ones, your higher self and the gods that will help you in your quest for truth. The eclipse will allow you to contact other worlds and other states of being."

Once the traffic began moving again, Tommy clicked the radio back off.

"Silly superstition shit." He said out loud.

It seemed as though it would be smooth sailing from there on out.

It was hot outside, so Tommy rolled down his window to feel the coolness of the breeze. But just as he was able to once again reach a speed of sixty-miles-per-hour, he came to a sudden stop. Traffic was stalled again. About twenty car lengths up the road, there had been an accident. He could see blue lights flashing up ahead and he could hear the sirens of oncoming emergency vehicles as they sounded louder and came into view.

"Damn it." He said to himself. And then he clicked the radio back on.

"As a piece of advice: Never cast spells during an eclipse. The outcome of the spells will be unpredictable because the Earth's natural energies and powers are loosened. It takes both a disciplined and experienced witch to harvest the power of eclipse magic. It is better to honor yourselves during these times or bring honor to the gods and other worldly beings."

"What the fuck?" Tommy exclaimed as he turned the channel.

"You are listening to channel 106.9 WFKM FM." The radio man said. "Stay tuned for another classic block of classic rock, right here on your classic rock station. 106.9 WFKM. It's twelve-seventeen in the afternoon and we're playing the music you love, music that taught us all how the night moves; a classic block of music from the legendary Bob Seger."

♫ "I was a little too tall, could've used a few pounds. Tight pants, point, hardly renowned. She was a black-haired beauty with big dark eyes, with points all her own, sitting way up high; way up firm and high." ♫

♫ "Out past the cornfields where the woods got heavy, out in the backseat of my sixty Chevy. We were working on mysteries without any clues. We were working on the Night Moves, trying to make some front-page drive-in news; working on the Night Moves, in the summertime, in the sweet summertime." ♫

Tommy checked the time again. It was now twelve-twenty in the afternoon.

"Tara," Tommy said as he heard her pick up the phone. "There's no way I'm going to be able to make it."

"Hi Tommy, this is Heather." She said. "Mom's outside. She asked me to keep a check on her phone. Hold on and I'll go get her for you."

Tommy waited and lit up a cigarette.

"Tommy," Heather said. "Mom says you better get here. It doesn't start until two-thirty, so she says please, please come."

"Okay," Tommy answered, "tell her I'm trying. And I hope to see you all soon."

Tommy was emotionally frustrated when he hung up the phone. She had been texting him night and day, but he hadn't seen her physically in three weeks or more.

"Out of the blue, she wants me to take off work and drive a hundred miles through intense traffic to watch the eclipse with her." Tommy thought to himself. "And I'll bet she's not alone."

Tommy took a long drag of his cigarette. It wasn't a hundred miles; it was only sixty. He was upset so he exaggerated to himself.

"Am I going to drive all the way, only to walk up to her house and find PJ and Michael standing there beside her?" He questioned.

He threw his cigarette butt out his window.

"Fuck, I don't like this." He said out loud. "I don't like this at all."

At one-forty-five in the afternoon Tommy pulled onto Tara's road. After almost four hours of driving, he was relieved the trip was over and that he had plenty of time to get there and visit before the event. As he turned into her driveway, the first thing he noticed was the red Volvo parked in the grass. She hadn't given him warning, but it hadn't been the first time. So, he instinctively prepared for whatever kind of confrontation would ensue.

Hope and Heather were swimming in the pool when he walked around the corner of the house, and hastily jumped out of the water and came running.

They both wrapped their wet arms around him excitedly as they said hello.

"We are so glad you could make it." Hope said smiling and dripping wet, the sun shone down upon her young glistening body that was barely covered by a small white bikini. "We've missed you so much." She said as she pulled him into her a little harder than she should have.

The girls then ran jovially back across the lawn and jumped with a splash back into the pool.

Michael was sitting in the shade of their covered back porch, watching his daughters and the other teenagers, who were bobbing up and down and splashing in the water. Tommy walked over and reached out his hand.

"Glad you could make it." Michael said as Tommy sat down on the chair beside him. "Tara's inside. She'll be out in a minute."

"It sure is a nice day out." Tommy said as they both turned their focus toward the sounds and the sights of the children swimming and splashing.

"Yes, it is." Michael answered.

Tommy watched as Michael got up quickly and walked over to the pool and peered down into the water.

"Stop it, Dad." Hope shouted. "You're being creepy."

Michael laughed as he ran back and sat back down in his chair.

"I never know what's going on here." He said. "The girls know more about what's really going on here than I do."

Tommy didn't answer. He didn't know how to.

Tara stayed inside the house for most of Tommy's visit.

When she finally came out, she was dressed for a funeral and said very little.

"I have to leave right after the Eclipse." Tara said as she pulled Tommy in for a kiss on his cheek. "My mom's sister died, and I'm supposed to pick her up at three. We'll share my glasses, so the eclipse won't damage our eyes."

"I was asked to drive all this way, only to spend my time on the porch with her husband, and then she's leaving right afterwards?" Tommy thought to himself. "Great." He thought sarcastically.

"Hey!." Michael shouted. "Get out of the water! It's time for the eclipse!"

Tommy was taken off guard by the shouting. He wasn't sure what the need was for the kids to be out of the pool to see the event. They could just as easily have watched it from inside the pool. But as they climbed out of the pool and stood barefoot upon the grass, he became keenly aware of the reason their dad had called them from the water, as he also gazed into the bright sunlight.

Just then, the girls and boys started singing. It wasn't a song that Tommy knew. And he could barely understand the words. But they were chanting. And they began to dance.

They were chanting, holding hands and dancing together in a circle.

They were laughing.

And they were giggling. And they were nearly naked in the grass.

"Maybe it's a song from their younger generation?" Tommy thought. "It's kind of like a rap song, maybe?" He thought again.

Suddenly, as the Moon passed between the Earth and the Sun, and the shadow made the daytime turn into night, the children dropped to their knees upon the grass and raised their hands and arms high up over their heads.

And they bowed down to the sun-god.

And they playfully prayed to the angels, the goddess of nature, and to the spirits of the air and the water and the trees.

Chapter Eight – Monsters in Her House

He hadn't been hallucinating. Or had he? To be perfectly honest, Tommy didn't know. He had seen them bow down with his own eyes. He had watched their parents' faces and saw only vacant stares coupled with subtle smiles. If these were his own children, he would have busted their asses. If this were just a childish game they were playing, it was still blasphemy.

They had just bowed down and prayed openly to a pagan god.

As he lay down upon his couch that afternoon, the scene played over and over in his mind. It couldn't have been real.

"It wasn't real." He thought. "My mind was playing tricks on me. This didn't really happen. It was just a childish game. They were all just acting silly and childish, and it didn't really happen."

He never talked with Tara about it. Something always seemed to come up.

She always seemed to have an excuse for them not to get together. And Tommy was growing tired of only texting.

He felt like he was banished indefinitely to the three by five text window, where all he saw were words.

The girls were starting school, or Michael had been in a wreck. It seemed anything and everything from their ATV being worked on to a dentist appointment that couldn't be rescheduled, came into play. Though, she continued texting him over the next two weeks consistently, especially during the early hours of the morning between one and three; the same hours he had seen the fire in the woods.

He would later remember that.

She texted him about her darkness and of the craziness she felt within her mind. She began sending him links to songs on YouTube. She told him of how these songs related to her innermost thoughts and feelings more completely, than any of her words ever could.

"I'm sorry if I've been so distant." She said. "But I'm in self-preservation mode. It's now almost to the day that I had my accident. I am almost the same age now that my mom was when her daughter was crippled and put in a wheelchair for life. And my daughter, Hope, is almost the same age that I was when everything happened."

Tara paused as Tommy listened.

"Needless to say, but I'm pretty fucked up right now. My inner voice tells me to smile and if questioned to deny, deny and deny." She continued. "It's how I've survived. It's all I know how to do."

She told him about Michael, and of how he had grown angrier towards her and their girls. She eluded his violent nature, his drinking heavily and his screaming. Though, she hadn't spoken of PJ in days.

"I'm scared of him, Tommy." She stated. "The girls are frightened of him, too. Michael's not the same man he once was." She related after a long pause. "Hope found a pistol that he had hidden in his room. It was loaded, and the safety was off." She continued. "It was my pistol, Tommy. It was my nine-millimeter pistol. He had stolen it from my room. I had it locked in my dresser. I have no idea how he got it open, and I have no idea when he took it."

At three o'clock later that same morning, Tara sent him a link to a very violent song.

The song was about monsters that were in her house or in her mind. The song's lyrics were maniacal. He couldn't remember the band's name that played it but the vocals were screaming and loud.

♫ You can't forget. The first time we met. You can't describe. What happened to you that night. You opened your eyes. And then realized. Nothing was what it seems. But I'm still with you in your dreams. 'Cause I am the monster in your mind. The reason for your sleepless night. I'm the monster in your head. Still waiting in your bed. Can't escape I'll be your fate. 'Cause I'm the monster in your mind. In your mind. You know I'm not real. Your mind still lets you feel. It's taking over. You're far from sober. It feels so right. The way we stay every night. ♫ - Broach – Fall to Rise

Tommy replied to her text immediately.

Tara didn't respond.

It worried him.

He tried calling her, but she still did not answer.

"Tara," He texted, "Tara, answer me."

Again, she did not answer.

Tommy waited in the darkness of his room while he sat at his bedside. The silence was deafening. His mind was racing. He began walking the floor, back and forth and up and down the hallway. He texted again at four o'clock, but there was still no answer, there was no reply.

At five-thirty in the morning he tried again, but again there was nothing.

Every possible scenario had been running through his mind. Michael had gone crazy. PJ had confronted Michael and the whole of the world had gone crazy. Someone has done something because she's said there were monsters in her house. She had told him of how these songs related to her innermost thoughts and feelings more than any of her words ever could.

He hadn't been able to sleep. His pulse was racing.

His imagination was running wild.

Tommy was panicking like a motherfucker..

"If I don't hear back from you by nine A.M., I'm coming over." He texted one last time.

At eight-fifteen in the morning, Tommy loaded his silver-plated derringer and his nine-millimeter pistol, and he placed them both on his passenger seat.

By this time, he had worked himself into a frenzy.

He was envisioning a crime scene, bloody walls and bodies on the floor. He saw himself walking into a horrific panorama of a morbid murder suicide.

His car tires slid in the gravel as he stopped suddenly in her driveway.

Tara's was the only visible car. He carried both guns. Susie and Bear didn't bark when Tommy pounded on her back door.

He peered through her windows.

There was no movement from the dark of the inside.

"Tara," Tommy texted. "Open the door, I'm outside."

"Tommy? What are you doing here?" Tara replied. "We had a late night. It's not a good time."

There was no blood.

There was no crime scene.

Her dogs weren't barking. Everything was calm.

Everyone had been asleep.

Tommy had overreacted.

"Fuck." He said as he exited her driveway. "What the fuck was I thinking? She's making me lose my ever-loving mother fucking mind."

The following evening, Tommy put aside his recent actions and reached out to Tara and asked her to dinner.

But she refused. She said she was tired, because she had been working again in the yard all day.

"Can we make it another time," She texted. "It's been a really bad week for me, and I just need to lie down and get some rest."

Tommy understood. He was upset, but he held it in, and he let it go.

It was the Facebook picture she posted at eleven o'clock that same night that set him off.

It was a beautiful picture of Tara in a baseball cap and jersey. She was sitting at a table in a local Mexican restaurant. She was smiling, and she looked like she was very happy.

Sitting beside her with his hand on her lap, was PJ. And he was smiling, too.

The caption read: "It is so good to get out and have some fun. It has been such a long time."

Tommy was racked with emotion.

He had been played. She had been playing him from the beginning.

"What about the date in the graveyard?" He said out loud. "Fuck. She's been fucking playing me like a god-damned fool."

Tommy knew he needed to take a step back. He needed to re-evaluate everything that had transpired over the last few months since his re-connection with Tara.

She was still married. Her husband was an abusive alcoholic with a heart condition and possible suicidal tendencies. And he still lived upstairs.

Michael also appeared to have unnatural desires for younger females, possibly, even his own daughters.

Tara had a lunatic friend who had told him that his wife was divorcing him because of her. While she had claimed he was ONLY her friend, she had shown him otherwise on numerous occasions.

Tara was amazingly beautiful, but she also had an elusive and darker side to her personality. She had jokingly spoken of a sexual threesome between her and her fourteen-year-old daughter, and her daughter's junior high-school volley-ball coach. And her daughter had also shown him a side of her, a view which Tommy never should have seen.

They had spoken in great detail of a new business venture, getting matching tattoos and of his moving into her adjoining guesthouse. They had looked at real-estate together and had discussed at great length her desires to move forward. Though, two months later, there had been no movement.

And they'd had amazing sex. He could never forget that.

But then, his tire had been slashed. He had lost two days of work and approximately three-hundred-dollars' worth in physical damages, and Tara had come to the defense of all possible suspects. And she had even alluded to him stabbing his own tire.

"Unbelievable." Tommy thought out loud.

Tommy also had wildly disturbing, socially taboo dreams the night of her fireworks party. It sickened him. And he

116

had awakened in a strange parking lot some twenty-four hours later without any knowledge of how he had gotten there.

And there was that moment on Heather's bed, when he could swear Hope had brushed her backside up against him in the twilight of the darkness. How could he ever forget that?

"And what was up with that Fuck-Wall?" Tommy thought. "What the fuck was up with that? And if the guitars that were strung upon her walls were made of gingerbread and candy-canes, it could have been that fucking Witches house in Hansel and Gretel.." He paused. But then his mind began drawing conclusions again. "There were monsters in her house, and a darkness she couldn't change. She admittedly claimed she was crazy."

He remembered everything his friend Seth had spoken to him about, regarding psychological disorders that accompany traumatic sexual abuse in children, especially girls under the ages of thirteen and fourteen-years-old.

He also recalled the dreams that were correlated between himself and his friend Raven. She was a medicine woman for her tribe, and she adamantly believed he was under a spell of some kind and was in extreme danger.

"What about Tara's maniacal texts of monsters in her house?" He thought. "I went to her house with loaded guns expecting a bloody crime scene."

117

Tommy got a cold beer out of his refrigerator and took a long drink. And then he stepped outside and lit up a cigarette.

"What about the fires in the woods?" He thought.

"There were people in black robes chanting around the flames." He thought further. "And I saw her children with my own eyes bowing down upon the grass and praying openly to the sun god.. And their mom and dad had said nothing.."

Tommy was now torn between what his spirit knew was happening, and what his mind wasn't fully allowing him to see. His heart still belonged to her as it fought through the pain of his current betrayal and the remorse of his promise long past.

And just then, something very dark crossed his mind. It had been there all along, though it had remained in the shadows, elusive, though omnipresent.

How many suicides had Tara been witness to?

She had called him by another man's name; a name of someone who had been close to her. His name was Henry, and she had been with him on the night of his death by suicide. Could it have been a coincidence? Michael's sister had also committed suicide.

And Tara had spoken of Michael's suicidal tendencies.

"Had there been others?" Tommy thought. "Could this darkness that Tara had spoken about be one of her sociopathic personalities that had homicidal predispositions?"

The possibilities were overwhelming.

And his conclusions were highly plausible and alarming.

"Could her darkness, her defensive personality, hate men with such malice aforethought, that she would cause them to die for her?" Tommy thought.

It would be untraceable, a perfect murder scene.

There would be no motive to believe anything other than death by suicide.

They would take their own lives of their own free will.

There would be no visible murder weapon.

There would be no blood-stained butcher knife.

And there would be no DNA to place her at the scene of the crime.

Could the love of Tommy's life have become a psychopathic killer?

"And Michael," he thought out loud to himself. "He's keeping Tara away from himself. He's denying her access because he's afraid of her." He continued. "He's being held prisoner. My God. He's just trying to stay alive."

Suddenly, the lyrics to a classic song by the Eagles played in his mind.

♫ "In the master's chambers, they gathered for the feast. They stab it with their steely knives, but they just can't kill the beast." ♫ Hotel California.

Chapter Nine – The Lake House

Autumn leaves fell peacefully, as he drove his car down the newly paved darkened side road. The leaves brought beautiful and brightened colors of yellows, reds and browns amidst the dark and paler shades of greens of the gently rolling pines, as they floated through the air and danced upon the winds.

The remote and artistically positioned A-frame home came into view as he rounded the bend. It sat facing outward towards a huge open lake. It was decorated with great open-bay windows and a large wooden deck that encircled the whole of the exterior, with staircases leading downward to a beautiful free-standing gazebo, with steps leading down from there to a scenic crossing bridge and a hand-carved wooden boat dock.

Bright red, white and pink balloons were tied with ribbons to the mailbox, as Tommy turned into Tiffany's driveway. He was the last to arrive. There were many cars aligning the gravel and still others parking upon the grass. He found a place to park in the back near the road and he grabbed his gift of homemade blackberry wine he'd brought for the occasion.

The Blackberry Wine was from his private wine collection. His favorite uncle on his father's side had handpicked the berries himself. When they had fermented, he distilled the berries into wine and placed the wine into thick green glass bottles. The label was an original, one of a kind, and it would never be able to be replaced. His uncle had died two years ago. And the unique vintage would no longer be made. But this occasion was worth sharing such an important part of his memories.

Tommy opened the back door of his car and grabbed his guitar case. And with the wine bottle in one hand and his guitar in the other, he walked through the rock driveway, around to the back deck and joined the party.

"TOMMY." Tiffany shouted. "I'm so HAPPY you made it."

Tiffany was wearing a pretty red tank-top that was opened like straps over her shoulders and arms, revealing her laced white bra beneath. She wore small white shorts that accentuated her tan complexion as she danced barefoot over to Tommy with a glass of wine in one hand and a smoking and lighted cigarette in the other.

She wrapped both of her arms around him, and she kissed him sweetly upon his lips.

Tiffany had been almost completely deaf since childhood, so the music being played on her BOSE stereo was incredibly LOUD.

"Make yourself at home." She shouted over the music. "I've got to go take a pee."

Tommy handed her the bottle of wine as she left him, and he sat his guitar case down by the wall behind the wicker sitting chairs. He didn't see anyone he knew, but it didn't matter. Most of the partygoers were twenty-something guys and girls who had already made themselves happy with drink.

Food was laid out upon two large tables: finger foods, sandwiches, potato chips and dips. A large grill smoked along the outside deck banister, manned by a shirtless guy wearing a baseball cap backwards.

"I guess I'm the odd man out." Tommy chuckled to himself. "These chic's are half my age, and the guys are ripped like football players."

Suddenly, a pretty scented girl rushed up from behind him and wrapped her arms around his waist. She nuzzled her face up against his back between his shoulder blades and began kissing him and nibbling him with her teeth.

"I have missed you so much." Meghan mumbled. "You smell SO good."

"Hello Meghan." Tommy replied without seeing her. "How've you been?"

Meghan let loose and grabbed him again from the front, pulling him into her and she kissed him passionately. Her nicely sized breasts pushed flatly up against his chest revealing the feel of her fully erect nipples, as her hands cupped his ass and squeezed him tightly.

"I'm going to fuck you tonight." She said matter-of-factually. "I'm going to fuck you so good."

Meghan was a beautiful twenty-something hottie. They had gone out a couple of times, and sex with her was amazing. But she had an obsessive side that had pushed him away and he had been leery of being around her.

"I'll have to control myself tonight." He thought to himself. "Because she's looking good, feeling good and she even smells good. I might just fuck the shit out of this girl, tonight."

"Tommy." Tiffany shouted. "I see you've found Meghan. Is she treating you alright?"

Tiffany didn't wait for an answer. She had brought three of her girlfriends with her and began introducing them to Tommy right away.

"Tommy, this is Mandi. She is one of my best friends and she's single." Tiffany stated as she smiled and winked at him. "And this is Cheyenne. She is Mandi's baby sister. She is very nice, and she is also single."

"Hello ladies." Tommy replied as they both came into him and gave him a warm embrace.

"And this is Jessica, she just turned twenty-one and she is a living doll." Tiffany related. "And oh, yes." She said as she pushed her closer to Tommy and pulled her long auburn hair back across her shoulders away from her face and held her chin up to meet Tommy's eyes. "She's single, too."

"Very nice to meet you, Jessica," Tommy said as he opened his arms to embrace her. Meghan didn't appear to be jealous. He noticed that.

All three of these youthful and attractive girls were playboy pretty. They were firm, and their breasts were perky, and they had beautiful youthful smiles. They were all three barefoot, tan, and they wore the shortest of shorts. Cheyenne revealed the sides of her boobs through her top while Mandi exposed her well-endowed breasts by way of her low-cut satin top. Jessica, the youngest, wore a black laced choker necklace and dressed more modestly. She was a college girl, and she had the cutest little freckles across her nose.

Tiffany made her excuses to mingle with her other guests. And someone brought Tommy a large crushed frozen Margarita with a line of salt around its brim, while he sat around a small, opened fire-pit upon the deck. And he conversed with these four incredibly attractive young women.

Everyone was drinking.

Everyone was flirting.

Tommy was having a really great time.

He wasn't sure how it all happened. One of the girls had mentioned going swimming in the lake. And the next thing he knew, they were all running down the wooden planks, past the Gazebo and across the bridge towards the water. Shorts and tops and bras were being taken off and dropped all along the way as four of the most gorgeous women he'd ever seen jump naked into the lake.

The sun had gone down behind the tree line, just enough to keep them hidden from any unwanted observers from the party.

Tommy stood at the edge of the dock and slipped out of his Calvin Klein's.

The waters of the lake glistened and shimmered as the girls splashed and made ripples. The lakes waters were high from a recent rain and crested only inches below the top surface of the dock.

The moment was almost mystical and surreal, and the lights from the stars and the moon shown down upon the waters. It was as though there were four beautiful mermaids, playing in the water, swimming up to him and resting their elbows upon the side of the dock.

It was still very early when they returned to the party some time afterwards, although most of Tiffany's guests had already left for the evening.

"I wondered where you guys had run off to." Tiffany said as she handed Tommy a glass of wine. "Did you guys go for a swim?"

"Yes," Tommy replied as the other girls went inside to change into something dry. "Great party," he said with a devilish smile.

"So," Tommy said as he took a sip of wine. "Where is this guy you've told me about? Am I going to get to meet him?"

"He got called away on business." Tiffany explained. "He wanted to be here, and he wanted to meet you, but he was called away at the last minute. When your boss needs you to support him at a million-dollar meeting in France, you drop everything and go, you know?" She said as she sipped her wine.

"Does he make you happy?" Tommy asked.

"Yes, he makes me very happy." Tiffany replied.

Tommy got up and opened his guitar case and took out his Takamine. As he started playing, Tiffany poured them two more glasses of wine.

"What about you Tommy?" Tiffany asked. "Are you seeing anyone? Is there anyone I should know about?"

The wine and the events of the night began to weigh heavily upon Tommy's mind. He was still hopelessly in-love with Tara. He didn't feel guilty about where he had just been, or what he had just done with the four girls down on the boat dock, but it didn't help his case any.

His emotions began to come to the surface as he heard Tiffany's question and as he began to play the strings of his guitar and sing. His eyes filled up with tears. One escaped and fell swiftly down his cheek. Tiffany stopped him and pulled him in close to her.

"Tell me what's going on." She consoled him. "I'm here for you and I care for you very much."

Tommy pulled out his phone and he showed her the picture.

"This is her," he said. "And that is him."

Tommy paused, as Tiffany reviewed the picture.

"Her name is Tara. And the guy is PJ." Tommy said in a mocking tone. "And he drives a big white truck." He said to emphasize PJ's need to over-compensate for the size of his dick.

Tommy went on to relate some of the issues he was having in his relationship with Tara. He was distraught.

And he openly wept. Tiffany consoled him as best she could. And she allowed him to confide in her.

"I don't know what I'm going to do." He related through tears. "I've loved this girl all my life. I don't understand how she could throw everything away over someone she told me was uneducated and very easy to manipulate."

Tiffany just held him.

"She told me he was stalking her." Tommy continued. "And that he had tried to violate her, in the daylight while her girls were in the yard. It's absolutely insane. I'm beginning to doubt my own eyes, ears and mind."

"It seems like everything you know about this guy, is what she's told you about him. Are you sure she's not manipulating you as well?" Tiffany suggested.

"Tommy," Tiffany continued. "Have you ever heard the saying that if you don't heal, you'll bleed on people who didn't cut you? Are you positive that PJ's the one who slashed your tire?

"I'm ninety-nine percent positive that he's the one who's responsible for putting a knife in my tire, yes." Tommy stated.

The conversation they'd had was private. It was only between Tommy and his friend, Tiffany. He was completely unaware that Meghan had stepped back outside, after changing into dry clothes, and had been eavesdropping upon their conversation the whole entire time.

As Meghan listened, she opened up her iPhone and she searched for Tara's and PJ's profiles on social media.

And then she found them.

"She's pretty for her age." She thought to herself. But when she pulled up PJ's picture on his profile page, she literally threw up a little in her mouth. "This will be easy." She thought to herself, "Too easy."

Meghan was manipulative, too. And she knew how to play the game.

Chapter Ten – Beneath the Twilight Skies

Once your eyes are opened to the evils of the world, you are never truly the same person again. When your psyche has been detrimentally traumatized, your inner being tends to compartmentalize your personality into multiple versions of one-self, and you surrender your free-will to the dominant authority.

The darkness was dominant. It was decisive, it was malicious, and its control was all-inclusive. It felt no guilt; no remorse and it offered no mercy. In its human form it was psychotic. In its spiritual form, it was demonic. But in its own eyes, it was the light. It was "the good", and all of the world, was evil.

The darkness rescued the weak, brought food and shelter to the homeless, and it liberated the unwanted from their human bonds. Those who were held captive by the treacherous chains of suppression, or those who were left abandoned and betrayed, sought refuge amidst the comfort of its hold.

The darkness offered enlightenment, knowledge, power and unimaginable pleasures. There were no limitations.

There were no forbidden fruits. It fed upon sacrificial desires, exposing one's soul, revealing one's secrets, and relieving one's pain.

Beneath the light of the crescent moon, they stood within the flowing waters and removed their garments. They embraced their coming freedom, and they relinquished the falseness of their vanities, and the oppression of their fallen masters, their shame, their brokenness and their anguish.

They cleansed their human forms with smoothly carved stones and the waters of life, as they stood upon their mother's earth beneath their feet.

They were runaways.

They had been abused.

They were unwanted and abandoned children.

There was nowhere left for them to run.

And they had nowhere else to turn.

They had gathered here beneath the flickering starlight that danced upon the waters, and they awaited their transformation.

"We welcome you, sisters and daughters." An angelic figure said as she waded into the waters like a ghost, let loose her clothing and joined the children in the coven circle. "You are loved. You are wanted. And you are home."

Some would become willing sacrifices, offering up their essence and releasing themselves from their human vessels. Others would be given unto loving servitude, where their young bodies would be glorified with intense pleasures, and they would be brought to orgasm again and again until they were truly enlightened by the coming light in the darkness. A select few would-be hand-chosen, the most beautiful and the most-pure, to carry the seed, of their new and loving masters.

The darkness did not turn a blind eye to the cannibalistic nature of the world of men. It had witnessed those eating babies and devouring their own young. It had also observed preteen mothers, who had been forced to do the same. It had watched in silence as the evil in man had carved up the living. And it had heard the cries and the horrifying screams, as the sacrifices watched their butchers cut the meat from their bodies and devour their own flesh and bone before them.

These were the same men who had set societal standards.

These were the same upstanding and righteous men who had dictated religiosity and supreme and authoritative morality upon the weak minded and the oppressed.

Religious atrocities and constitutional right had delivered the children of man into world-wide child sex-slave trafficking while the submissive and the passive had turned away.

"These men are the epitome of evil," whispered a calming voice amidst the waters. "But society calls them good." The voice continued. "They can no longer hurt you. And you should no longer fear them. We have all been soothed and appeased. We have all been made indifferent, and we have all been numbed asleep. But soon," the voice paused, "all eyes will be opened."

The truth it seemed …was a lot like poetry, and everybody hated poetry.

Suddenly, the echo of music broke the tranquility of the night, as it filled the air and encircled the whole of the forest, and the rivers and the trees.

♫ "Please allow me to introduce myself; I'm a man of wealth and taste. I've been around for a long, long year, stole many a man's soul and faith. And I was 'round when Jesus Christ, had his moment of doubt and pain. I made damn sure that Pilate washed his hands and sealed his fate. Pleased to meet you. Hope you guess my name. But what's puzzling you is the nature of my game." ♫

The children sang.

And the children played.

And they splashed upon the waters of the darkness.

They were free.

They were home.

And they danced beneath the twilight skies.

♫ "Just as every cop is a criminal, and all the sinner's saints. As heads is tails just call me Lucifer, 'Cause I'm in need of some restraint. So, if you meet me have some courtesy, have some sympathy, and some taste. Use all your well-learned politesse? Or I'll lay your soul to waste, um yeah. Pleased to meet you, hope you guessed my name." ♫ Sympathy for the Devil – The Rolling Stones

Chapter Eleven – The Gathering Storm

She sat beneath the shade of her large oak tree, beside the stone statue of her winged angel. The breeze was cool and refreshing as the winds whipped through its branches, causing the autumn leaves to loosen their hold and fall gently upon the grass beneath her feet and onto her lap. She was revitalizing her spirit. It was the dawn of a beautiful sunrise, a wonderful new beginning and a peaceful Sunday morning.

Tara hadn't heard from Tommy in several days. He had made himself distant and he had begun displaying tendencies that she did not like. He had become incredibly jealous of her friend, and he had told her so.

He had also gotten angry with her when she had told him of the security cameras, and of what they had captured on the day his tire had been flattened.

She had begun to doubt the tire incident was anything more than a nail he had run over, and a dramatic episode he had concocted to drive a wedge between herself and PJ. She knew PJ had nothing to do with it. He was an ignorant buffoon, but he wasn't that stupid. And Michael hadn't shown one ounce of jealousy in almost ten years.

He wouldn't have done it either.

The whole ordeal had become more drama than what she was prepared to put up with, and it had also become a focal point between herself and Tommy. It was the moment when everything had started to go wrong.

He had become belligerent, argumentative, jealous, and he had even pounded on her door one early morning brandishing loaded weapons.

It hurt her deeply when he referred to Michael as "the little boy who lived upstairs." What right did he have to make fun of Michael, or the situation? And he also had called PJ a Neanderthal, a stalker and a physically abusive person. She got upset every time Tommy brought up his big white truck, because she knew he was referring to PJ's overcompensation for his small sized penis.

"Tommy is becoming very mean and hateful." Tara thought. "He's not the same as I remember him being when we were kids together."

PJ, on the other hand, had become the perfect gentlemen.

He brought her coffee and breakfast in the mornings, and they'd often sit together and watch the sunrise from her back porch. He helped her weed the lawn on numerous occasions and he had always been there at a moment's notice when anything needed to be fixed or worked on.

He was strong, and he had the physical capabilities to lift her when the situation called for it. He never said anything out of the way or judgmental to her, and he had never called Tommy a bad name, the whole time he had been in the picture.

Sure, Tommy had once brought her and her girls' breakfast. He had even included gifts for her and her girls in the bag that he'd left on her back porch swing. And he had also sent her flowers. They were beautiful. But she felt they were given to her as a way of making up for his recent actions. She didn't believe they were given sincerely, or that his intentions were genuine.

PJ was enjoying the show. And he hated that motherfucker.

The more he played his cards right and did nothing, the less competition he had. He knew better than to say anything. So, he kept his mouth shut.

Instead of saying anything out loud and pushing her away, he allowed Tara to overreact and over-exaggerate the smallest of issues, until she'd worked herself into a cluster of self-doubt, self-righteousness and self-preservation.

He wouldn't have to do anything other than play nice and be the good guy.

Eventually, he knew his dumb-ass competition would do something really stupid and then, not only would he win Tara's affection, but he would also win over her girls.

And that alone would earn him his spot in their mothers' bed.

Besides, Tara didn't know everything. He knew she thought he was dumb.

But he could be smart when he wanted to. And he was really smart when it came to women.

Tara didn't know about the woman who tended the bar down by the truck stop, he'd been talking to her for months. And she didn't know about the little brunette who waited tables on Tuesday nights, down at the diner in Marion Springs. She had a nice ass and a gorgeous pair of tits. There had also been a random hot chick recently, who had been flashing her tits and ass at him on instant messenger. He would like to fuck her too. Tara definitely didn't know about her.

"What the fuck?" PJ said to himself. "I'm getting more offers for pussy now than I ever did."

Meghan had been messaging PJ. She had been flirting with him and sending him suggestive pictures. They weren't pictures of her body. She had more sense than that. She had put up bogus pictures on a lesser used profile and had been trying to get him to meet with her locally or to give her any form of inclination that could prove she was right.

Meghan thought Tommy was amazing. She didn't know if it was love. But she loved to fuck him, and that was close enough. Not only did she find him incredibly handsome, masculine and attractive, but she was also drawn to his youthfulness, his vigor, his raw stamina and his natural energy. He was also more sensual than any other man she had ever fucked.

He was a singer; a songwriter and he had also written and published several books. She loved his touch.

Tommy was wonderful, in every sense of the word. And everyone who knew him loved him. But this dumb bitch had captured his heart. And it was tearing her apart.

She hoped PJ would say something she could use against him. She wanted him to admit that he and Tara were lovers. Once he had done that, she could then rush back into Tommy's arms. It wouldn't exactly have the same result as the Florence Nightingale effect, but, no matter what the outcome, she was going to find out if there was anything truly going on between that old bitch and that hillbilly redneck.

Meghan didn't understand why she felt the need to compete with a woman who was obviously twice her age.

She was old. And she also had to be bat-shit-crazy for choosing a retarded looking guy over Tommy. Not only that, but she was also in a wheelchair.

"A guy would have to do a shit-ton of work to have sex with her." She said out loud as she perused Tara's profile page. "I totally fucking don't get it. I mean, I really don't fucking get it at all."

She had never met Tara. And she never wanted to. But she already hated her.

Hope and Heather were getting good grades. And they had both made a lot of new friends recently. Hope had joined the cheer leading squad, while Heather had gotten into creative writing.

They both honestly missed Tommy. They really liked him. He was funny and talented and obviously cared for them and their mom very much.

They didn't understand what had been happening lately, but they knew something was up, because PJ had been coming around more and more often and had been sitting with their mom on the back porch late at night and talking with her.

Neither one of them liked that. Because neither one of them liked PJ. Hope could not see herself getting close to him. And Heather was still confused by her feelings for Tommy and her loyalty to her dad. PJ was just an extra added thorn in her side.

They both wished he would go away.

Tommy did his best to stay away. If Tara texted him, he would answer. But he would keep his answers short, and he would keep his emotions distant.

Too many strange and abnormal events had occurred.

And, they had happened consistently. He'd begun to not only question his own sanity but also, he'd begun to doubt his own eyes.

He needed to see the donkey-faced tree again. And he wanted to investigate the area where the dark ones had built the fire that night. This time however, he wouldn't venture through the woods in the dark; he would go and see it in the daylight. He was a grown man, but he didn't want to see it alone. He needed a second set of eyes. He needed a witness. So, he called a friend for backup. And he did his best to explain the situation.

"Sarge, if it was only one thing I could dismiss all of it." Tommy related. "But when I look at it as one solid puzzle with many smaller pieces, the picture I see is unimaginable. I don't believe it, and I'm the one telling you about it. Bring your guns and ammo. We really need to check this out."

Sarge and Tommy had been friends since their freshman year in high school.

He was a military vet, a conservative theorist and a believer in government conspiracies. He had gone by the name 'Sarge,' since Operation Desert Storm. He was also a friend of Tara's. He had known her since high school as well, and he had also helped Tommy fix her HVAC air-conditioning system last month when he'd asked him for his assistance.

147

"This is really fucked up." Sarge said. "You know that, right?" He questioned. "You really think Tara's a witch?"

"I don't know what the hell I believe at this point man." Tommy answered. "I know I've been riding a psychological roller-coaster these fast few months. And I know I have seen things that are NOT normal." He continued. "And I saw her girls bow down at the lunar eclipse and pray to the sun-god. I saw it man. I really saw it."

"I believe you brother." Sarge stated. "Now, tell me about this donkey-faced tree."

"I saw a fire in the woods. I grabbed my loaded pistol, and I walked through the darkness and the weeds to the base of grass that grew between the creek bed ahead of me and the wood line of trees and brush where I stood in the shadows." Tommy related. "Ahead of me there was a huge fire. I counted twelve people donning shiny black hooded robes. They were singing, chanting and they began to dance. The light from the fire flickered off the old tree I was leaning against. And the motherfucker had eyes man. I swear to God that motherfucker had eyes."

"It sounds like we're going to have some fun." Sarge said enthusiastically.

He knew Tommy well. And if he said the tree had eyes, then he believed him. Whether or not Tara was a witch, he'd have to determine that for himself, but he believed the circumstances and events that his friend had related, warranted extra review and caution.

"You'll have to drive." Tommy said, "Because they know my car. And we'll need to park at the bridge and walk through the creek. It'll be about a mile long walk."

"I'll pick you up, in the morning." Sarge stated. "Let's make it happen."

Chapter Twelve – The Donkey Tree

At sunrise, the sounds of running waters and awakening life beneath the trees were refreshing. The air was crisp, and the coming light amidst the vanishing shadows, beckoned them on-wards.

The cradle of water exhibited shallow streams, with large branches of drift-wood and dry creek-rock, as they tread along its twisting path quietly.

Deer season opened last Saturday with the start of a one-hundred-thirty-six-day archery season. The crossbow, youth gun, muzzle-loader and modern gun seasons followed later in the fall.

Sarge carried his large handmade archery-bow and arrows with an animal-skin strap over his left shoulder.

His two smaller handguns were kept tactfully concealed in their holsters, while he carried his rifle in both hands.

It was a Barrett REC7 AR-15 semi-automatic rifle.

Tommy carried his nine-millimeter pistol and his silver-plated derringer.

Though they were both decked out in pale green camouflage and mud boots as they walked along the creek bed, Sarge was prepared to take something down.

"We had a good crop of acorns last fall, and a mild winter followed by a wet spring and summer," Sarge said. "We should see some deer if we can stay down wind of them."

Tommy had no interest in hunting deer. And he knew his friend was only talking about wildlife to keep them both calm. He would hunt deer if he had to eat or to feed his family, but he never hunted for sport.

"Whatever is happening in these woods," Tommy thought. "It is a totally different kind of animal."

Up ahead, they could hear a loud rushing of water. The small creek had widened. And the stream had collected into a pool where it had become much deeper, and you could no longer see the bottom for the algae and the moss that had colored it a rich shade of green.

They waded through the cool flowing waters up to their knees, and up to the precipice, where a small and charismatic waterfall had formed. A cascade of running water fell from a vertical drop over the smooth, though rocky ledge.

The colors of gold and crimson sparkled in the morning sunlight, and then became absorbed by the deep green foliage-colored waters below.

From their height, they could see a steep descent of the river. Though the water seemed to have no exit from its prison, they could see the sand and stone formed by the erosion of bedrock from turbulent rainstorms further downstream. There was an opening in the tree line, a natural phenomenon or a well-designed singularity amidst the trees.

"You first," Sarge said as he laughed and pointed downward over the waterfall.

"No, ladies first," Tommy answered smiling and nodding his head.

"No, I insist." Sarge chided him, "Age before beauty."

"You're older than I am, you mother-fucker." Tommy said jokingly.

"Yes, but I'm prettier." Sarge said with a wink.

They exited the stream and continued on their expedition following the creek-bed. And they descended the rocky and weed-filled terrain carefully.

"Watch out for copperheads." Sarge stated. "Those little bastards are mean, and they'll sneak up on you."

Both Sarge and Tommy were judging their position in relation to where Tara's home was located. By their calculations, they would be parallel to her driveway in about two-hundred yards. At that point, they would, by Tommy's estimation, have about a fourth of a mile to travel.

Coincidentally, it would place them precisely at the opening of the tree line.

"This is the place." Tommy said. "Let's stop here for a minute or two. We should be directly across from Tara's house. And I need to light up a smoke."

"That's a good idea." Sarge stated as he found a large stone and sat down. "I don't know if you've heard anything, but there is something out here with us. It's been following us."

"Don't try to scare me, Sarge." Tommy said as the hairs began to stand up on his arms and at the base of his neck. "I'm serious."

"I'm not shitting you." Sarge stated as a matter of fact. "Listen and be very still."

They both sat quietly in the shelter of the wooded landscape. And they listened intently, while Tommy exhaled puffs of bluish smoke. And there came a foul smell of urine in the morning air.

"Did you hear that?" Sarge asked. And then, before Tommy could answer, he placed his finger to his lips and said, "Quiet, it came from over there." He continued as he pointed behind where he and Tommy were resting.

Tommy's eyes grew as wide as saucers, as Sarge raised his weapon and peered through its scope.

There came a loud rustling sound.

It sounded big.

He could hear his friend release the safety and cock the hammer back.

The forest became eerily quiet.

And then they heard the howl.

It was a sound like no other they'd ever heard; a jackal, a hyena, and the cry of a wolf all mixed together.

Sarge saw its face, though he would not describe it to his friend until much later, after they had exited the woods. It had peered out through the branches of the trees, and it had looked into his eyes. The eyes were a yellow amber in color and its face was canine shaped. And it had long pointy ears like the breed of a Doberman Pincher.

His mind tried to associate its appearance with any and all other known animals, but he couldn't. It stood upright on its hind legs like a man, seven or eight feet tall.

And although it remained mostly hidden behind the heavy bushes, weeds and trees, he could see it had extremely long arms and long fingers.

It wasn't a bear. It wasn't a dog. And it had smiled.

"That wasn't a mother-fucking Bigfoot either." He rationalized in his mind.

There came a loud popping sound, like that of bones cracking.

"What the hell was that?" He said out loud as another creature descended from the trees and landed on all fours beside the other. They could hear them grunt and huff, as though they were frustrated.

Then a yipping sound resounded from further back in the woods. And the beasts scurried away fast, and heavily, through the brush and the weeds of the forest.

"What was that?" Tommy asked.

"You don't want to know." Sarge said. "And I don't want to know either." He continued. "There were three of them. Two were there behind us. One had circled around from the front. We were being hunted. Let's get moving so we can find out what's going on with that donkey-tree and get the hell out of these woods."

"I'm right there with you." Tommy agreed.

Both Sarge and Tommy continued their journey, through the thickened wood and brush and weeds.

Suddenly, Tommy's phone vibrated and resounded with a ding.

"Where are you?" Tara's message read. "How've you been?"

Tommy paused before answering.

"It's her." He said to Sarge. "She's got eerily disturbing timing."

"Go ahead and answer her." Sarge insisted. "We're almost done. Just, for the love of God, don't tell her where we are."

"I'm doing, alright." Tommy texted back.

"Good. I'm glad." Tara instantly replied. "If you're not busy this Saturday, maybe you could stop by?" She related, but before Tommy could respond, she texted again. "Maybe you could bring your friend Meghan with you?"

Tommy froze.

"What the fuck?" He said out loud.

He didn't reply back. He knew instantly that Meghan had just fucked something up. She may have just fucked everything up.

"I'm in the middle of the mother-fucking woods, trying to find out about this damn donkey-faced tree, and now this shit." He exclaimed. "Fuck. Fuck. Fuck. Fuck." He said as he stomped his feet on the ground.

"What happened?" Sarge asked.

"I don't know, but Tara somehow knows Meghan." He explained. "And nothing good can come from that." "So, tell me." Sarge replied. "Did you fuck Tara?"

Tommy thought about his answer.

And then he said, "Does a gentleman say yes, or no to that question?"

"Did you fuck her?" Sarge said sounding out each word individually.

"We got together once in high school." Tommy related. "And we've gotten together a few times since we became re-acquainted."

Tommy paused.

"But you know?" Tommy continued. "I believe I'm the one who's just got fucked." He paused again. "I don't have time for this bullshit." He said as he led the way to the clearing. "Let's get some answers so we can get out of here. I'll deal with this shit later."

They continued on. And they entered the clearing. It was just as Tommy had remembered and described. The creek turned sharply to the right and the field of green grass lay between the water and the tree line to his left. They walked to the center of the secluded meadow, and they examined the circle of ash and burnt wood.

There had been a recent fire. And the grass had been freshly mowed.

Buried in the ground like a walkway, were smoothly carved stones. They were laid out purposefully and precisely, in a completed shape of a pentagram, with the fire pit at its center.

One lone standing oak stood tall across the meadow, with a large skull of an unknown animal secured by rusted nails to its base. It wasn't like the skull of a bull or the skull of a deer. It was extremely large, and it was more closely related to that of a canine.

"This is some devil shit, man." Sarge stated. "We need to get the fuck out of here right now."

Tommy agreed. But he wasn't going back through those woods. He knew the way out. He motioned for Sarge to follow as he entered the wooded brush that led out to the road.

"This is the tree." He said to Sarge as they quickly walked past it. "I wasn't lying, was I? The motherfucker had eyes, didn't it?"

"Yes." Sarge agreed.

But they weren't the scariest things that he'd seen that morning.

As they walked briskly down the road to Sarge's vehicle, Tommy pointed out PJ's truck in Tara's driveway.

"I'm done with this shit man." Tommy exclaimed. "She's lied to me from the beginning and I'm telling you, she's into some witch shit, man. I haven't told you half of it."

"When we get back to my truck, I'll run you home." Sarge stated. "And then, later tonight, we can meet back up and have some drinks. After we process everything we've seen this morning, we can talk about it." He continued. "And you can tell me everything."

Tommy smoked a cigarette as they walked.

Sarge kept watch through the woods with his rifle still cocked and loaded.

He thought about the face that he'd seen between the trees, and he remembered the creature's howl. He also reflected upon the pentagram and the large skull that had been nailed to the base of the tall oak in the meadow.

It hadn't been a face of a donkey that he'd seen on the tree his friend had pointed out, either.

It did have ears.

And it did have eyes.

But it didn't have an equine or bovine nose.

It was canine. It was the skull of a very large dog.

"I need to ask you something." Sarge stated as they walked. "Have you ever heard …of the Dog-Man?"

Chapter Thirteen – The Descendants of Adam

The waning moon was luminescent, as the wood from the fire crackled and popped. The flames ascended higher, as the smoke grew thicker and twirled into the night amidst the translucent sky. A gentle wind cooled the air, and as the star-filled heavens blackened, the outline of clouds moved slowly, appearing effervescent.

From his back-porch, Tommy sat in his chair upon his wooden deck, stoked the fires from the pit, and peered out into the vastness of space.

Sarge sat between the shadows and the flickering light, and he drank a cold Budweiser.

"That was some serious shit we saw this morning." Sarge said, breaking the silence. "It's not that I didn't believe you, I did, but it's hard enough believing it when you see it with your own eyes."

"Exactly," Tommy replied. "It's cognitive dissidence. When we suddenly learn a truth that changes our whole way of thinking, our brains go into overdrive, and we try to rationalize it away; because we want a constant 'Normal.'" He continued. "It becomes a moment like in the movie, the Matrix; take the blue pill, go back to sleep and wake up and everything is the way it was. But take the red pill, and you open your eyes to the real world and find out just how far down the rabbit hole goes."

"So, you have heard of the Dog-Man, correct?" Sarge asked.

"Yes, my buddy Seth and I have spoken about them at length." Tommy replied. "We've even discussed going to the Land between the Lakes and doing some hunting."

"You won't have to go that far." Sarge replied. "That's what those things were in the woods this morning. The skull on that Oak tree, that wasn't from a Brahman Bull or a Buck Deer. That skull was from a large canine. And it wasn't from a larger sized wolf or coyote." He continued. "And Tommy, that wasn't a donkey-faced tree that you showed me, either. It wasn't a horse's nose or a cow's nose. The face was that of a dog, a very large dog."

Sarge paused while Tommy contemplated and stared into the fire.

"It was a Dog-Man." Sarge confirmed.

Reports of dog-headed men could be traced back to Egyptian antiquity.

Anubis was the Egyptian god of the dead and he protected the route to the afterlife. He was usually depicted with the body of a man and the pointy-eared, narrow-muzzled head of a jackal.

In ancient civilizations, dog-faced men were the most worshiped divine beings. Their supernatural mystique offered evocative imagery of magic and brutality, which was deemed characteristic of bizarre people of distant places, and their tales kept returning to medieval literature.

Some believed they were mortal and rational animals.

While others believed they were part god, or part human, and therefore, direct descendants of Adam.

"My friend," Sarge said. "You need to stop all forms of communication with Tara, right now. I haven't seen everything that you have. And I don't know everything that you know. But I do know what I've seen with my own eyes. And I believe everything that you've told me is the truth." He continued. "She has a way about her, she always has. She draws men to her naturally."

"She's be-witching." Tommy stated as he looked deeply into the flames.

"Damn right." Sarge agreed. "And how can she look as young as she did in high school? I'm not saying it's a bad thing, I'm just asking, how?

"It is uncanny." Tommy agreed.

The fire in the pit began to smolder, so they gathered more wood as they discussed the situation further.

Tommy laid a large dry piece of timber upon the flame and sparks flew high into the air. Then they both popped the top open on a cold beer, and Tommy began to tell Sarge everything.

It was two-forty-seven in the morning when he had finished. Sarge had been listening closely and processing all of it: the abusive childhood, the guitars on the wall, the lies, the Fuck-wall, the dreams and the eclipse.

"Did her girls really bow down and pray to the sun-god?" Sarge asked. "Right out in the open, and their mom and dad said nothing?"

"Yes, they did," Tommy confirmed. "I saw them bow down and Tara and their dad didn't say anything. It was eerie and surreal."

"Even if there wasn't any of this other shit going on," Sarge said. "Any normal person, especially a Christian, wouldn't have allowed that shit. That is blasphemy."

Suddenly, Tommy's phone lit up and resounded with a ding.

"Hey brother, you up?" Seth's text message read.

Tommy hit the dial button.

"Hey man, what's going on?" Tommy said when he answered.

"I didn't know if you'd be up." Seth replied.

"Yes, I'm sitting outside on the back porch with Sarge, and we've got a fire going and we're having some beers." Tommy stated. "I'll put you on speaker phone."

"Hey Sarge," Seth replied, and they both exchanged pleasantries. "Listen Tommy, have you seen what Tara has just put on social media?"

"No," Tommy answered. "What did she post?"

"She's calling someone out brother." Seth replied. "I didn't know if it was about you or what, but she's calling on her 'Coven of Witches,' brother. And they're talking about murder, right in the open on social media."

"What the fuck?" Tommy replied. "What did she say?"

"Check it out man." Seth stated. "And you know that guy who was convicted of murder, that Rowan guy?"

"Yes," Tommy answered. "We were in the band together in high school. And Tara told me they had been close friends. She'd even said that she had visited him in prison after he was convicted of murder, and that she'd kissed him on the cheek. She'd also said she'd been the last girl he'd ever kissed."

"Well," Seth stated. "He replied to her post, too. And he's a murderer. He killed that girl with a sword twenty some years ago, in the toy soldier museum, remember? And he was sentenced to prison. She's calling the dark forces to her my friends. And they're swearing their

167

allegiance to her. She's openly calling for murder in an open forum."

Sarge pulled her profile up on social media. And he read it out loud as both Seth and Tommy listened.

"In a war you created, with a person you don't know, to stalk my child's account for information to use as ammunition is unforgivable." Sarge read out loud. "Dig deep and try to find just a shred of decency and self-respect, please. My children are off limits to you. I will kill you and sleep like a baby before I let you hurt them."

"See," Seth confirmed. "I told you. Now, read the comments below her post. She's calling on her 'Coven of Witches,' and they're openly condoning her words and vowing their support."

Sarge reviewed the comments and started reading them out loud one by one.

"The next comment reads," Sarge related. "As the saying goes …friends help you move; good friends help you move the bodies. Consider me a great friend. All you have to do is point."

"And the one below that reads," Sarge continued. "I am proficient in shoveling."

"Read the one from the convicted murderer." Seth said over the phone speaker. "It's insane."

"All you have to say is 'who'. Better if you say 'where.'" Sarge read out loud. "Things have a way of resolving themselves if 'forces of nature' come into play. We grew up apart from each other just across the way. I always fancied you ...yet I seemed insufficient for your purposes. Still, you have my loyalty. Just tell me who needs to be 'corrected'. This I can still do." Sarge continued reading. "Just let me know what I can do for you and your baby ...I have little else to lose. I will always be grateful to you for what you gave me in my hour of need. Before I descended into HELL, you were there for me – this I will never forget."

"This is fucking crazy." Sarge stated as they all reflected upon the words.

"The chic is psycho." Seth said over the speaker phone. "Tommy, we've talked about it before. The girl you loved is still there, but so are the other twenty-five or thirty personalities. She's trapped inside somewhere and unless she gets some psychological help from professionals, to help identify them and put them back together in her consciousness, she's lost man."

"And" Sarge interjected, "with all this devil shit and witchcraft going on, including the kids bowing down at the lunar eclipse, the pentagram and dog-man skull ...and the tree, there's nothing you can do."

"Do you think she's been killing people?" Tommy asked.

"You said there were several suicides that she had either witnessed or had been close to people who had died that way, correct?" Seth asked and then he continued. "There is a huge possibility that she is a serial killer. She may have been killing people since high school."

"Oh," Seth said before anyone could say anything. "Did I hear someone say something about a pentagram and a dog-man?"

Sarge related the story of their adventure to Seth as Tommy listened.

"I've never seen anything like them before." Sarge exclaimed. "They looked like one of those werewolves from that movie back in the eighties, the Howling." He continued. "Once you see these things in real-life, it's like, it's like it fucks you up. I drew down on one with my rifle, but they didn't charge, so I didn't fire. Honestly, after all I've read about other sightings, I don't know if I could have stopped them."

"It's a good thing you didn't shoot." Seth stated. "In Louisiana they're known as the Rougarou. They're essentially bayou-dwelling werewolves and they're prominent in Cajun folklore. Some know them as Skunk apes, Grass men or Boogers." Seth continued. "Highly trained soldiers, covert operations specialists have been sent by the U.S. military into areas that are deemed to be occupied by legions of these creatures. But, they have either come up missing, or, they have been killed themselves. You just don't hear about it. It's not reported by the liberal media."

"Seth," Sarge stated. "Did Tommy tell you about the donkey-tree?"

"Yes." Seth answered.

"Well, it wasn't the face of a donkey." Sarge corrected. "It was a dog-man."

"Wow." Seth exclaimed. "That's fucked up. That's really fucked up."

"Tommy," Sarge said, changing the subject. "I was just thinking; does she know where you live? Did you ever tell Tara where you live or bring her over to your house?"

"Never," Tommy answered. "As far as I know, she doesn't know where I live. But, she does have ...your ...address. She asked for it, remember, so she could send you a thank you card for helping fix her HVAC system?"

"Fuck." Sarge exclaimed. "I remember now. But you know ...she never sent me a card."

"I wonder why she'd asked for it then." Seth stated questioningly. "Be careful Sarge, seriously."

Tommy stoked the fire again, and a rush of flame and sparks lifted up into the air. It was getting colder out as the dew began to fall. And he and Sarge scooted up closer to the fire for warmth.

"Did you see this one?" Sarge asked as he returned to viewing the social media posts. "It's on one of Rowan's posts. Listen to this." He said as he began to read again out loud. "Tara, do you remember how much I cared …even with Dan and the others. I know I am not much, but I am still able to react with what are considered 'humans.' If you have problems still …just simply 'talk' to me. I am your friend homegirl."

"And here is her reply." Sarge stated as he read again. "Of course, I remember. You were my first official love interest." Tara replied with a winking emojis. "The first person, ever, truly, who saw me as beautiful. I was such an ugly duckling. That was a long time ago, a lifetime ago. I will never think of you and not remember one overloaded inner tube meeting violently with a tree. And just everything we did in the youth group. You are my family, you know, that right?"

"It sounds like a love-fest." Seth stated.

"Oh, and here's what he said back to her." Sarge stated as he continued reading. "To me, YOU were NEVER ugly. We grew up together across the hill and I always saw you, in my mind and heart, as 'beautiful'. It was I who was not worthy – Jeff and all. I just had to give up on you because I thought I was not what you wanted. The CHAIR was never an issue …I was. I NEVER wanted to embarrass you. You just never seemed to be interested in me that way. But …I went to HELL. You were free to pursue 'life'. I was condemned to live my 'death'. But I am now 'free' to do as I wish. Whether I am worthy of consideration is up to you. No pressure, just fact. I will be your friend regardless. I am sorry for your sorrow …we all have it. I have nothing left to lose. And …in my own way, I will always love you, even if you never feel the same."

They all sat quietly for a moment after Sarge had finished reading, and they reflected upon everything that had transpired.

"Guys," Tommy said. "If this were a novel, and I was a character in the book, what role would it be that I've been playing?"

"From my point of view, Tommy," Seth stated. "She brought you in like a lamb, and she's trying to devour you like a lion." Seth continued. "She made you fall in-love with her all over again, and then she made you witness to things, you were threatened, and then she pushed you away. To be honest with you brother, I believe she's been grooming you, like a predator. While she made you believe that you were the leading character in her romance novel, she's really cast you in the role of the sacrificial lamb."

"Wow, that's deep." Sarge interjected. "But I agree. You are in danger."

Tommy placed the last parcel of wood, for the night, on the fire.

"Hypothetically speaking," Tommy stated. "What happens now? Will I be replaced? I mean, will someone new be cast in my current role?"

"Hypothetically speaking, yes," Seth answered, and Sarge agreed. "This type of behavioral personality is consistent and methodical. There is an order to chaos, a method to madness. She needs a willing victim; someone who comes to her and surrenders willingly. It's a systematic process. And it has to be someone who loves her."

"Should we contact the police?" Tommy asked.

"We don't have any evidence of anything happening, no murders and no crimes." Sarge stated. "Currently, all we have is circumstantial possibilities."

"I agree. We only have hypothetical theories." Seth interjected. "We don't even have any proof that a crime has been committed."

Tommy thought hard, and he tried to formulate his next sentences.

"What if Rowan was innocent of murder, all those years ago," Tommy stated, "and, he had taken the fall for Tara?"

Tommy slowly devised his thoughts as he stirred the ashes of the fire.

"And, what if Rowan," He continued, "is taken back into her fold, and ends up dying instead of me?"

The night grew eerily quiet and still, as they contemplated the implications.

Then, Tommy poured water over the reddish-orange embers.

Smoke rushed upwards from out of the pit.

And the flames went out.

Chapter Fourteen – A Desire for Sacrifice

The walls were barren, and the room was empty and void.

Cardboard boxes were stacked and over-flowing in the middle of the floor as she swept the dust from the baseboards, and from out of the corners. The decorative curtains had been taken down, leaving the double paned windows open and exposed to the view from the outside.

It was raining heavily. And the sounds of the water falling and hitting upon the glass echoed throughout the apartment.

Everything that she had tried to do had gone wrong. She had only flirted with the guy to gain information because she wanted Tommy back. But it had escalated. Tommy had yelled at her. And now, her life was being threatened.

Meghan couldn't believe it would ever turn out this way. How could she have known? She had no idea how badly her single flirtatious gesture could spiral out of control the way it had. The old woman was evil. And one of her loyal followers was a convicted murderer, who had vowed his devotion to her and had sworn to kill for her.

It was insanity.

She would clean until the rains had stopped. And then, with the help of a few of her remaining friends, she would load the rest of her belongings into the U-Haul van, and she would leave. She had family in Indiana.

They would make room for her until she got back on her feet. And it was far enough away to elude the craziness and re-build her life and feel safe again, after the recent death threats against her.

She'd had to move before. She was used to it. She wasn't even legally in the United States. She was from Venezuela. And thank God, she hadn't been using her real name.

Michael stood in his bedroom looking out through his opened window.

The rain hit his face, but he did not care. He had been served divorce papers. And, he had been asked to leave.

An explosion of thought, mixed with the disillusion of a failed attempt at a happy marriage, family and a loving home-life had broken him.

He had gotten angry. And he had become violent. He had made the ones he loved more than anything in the world …cry and scream at him. He wanted it all to end.

He wanted it all to be over.

He thought about killing himself, as his sister had done before him. It would be better for everyone. Perhaps he would hang himself. It would be quick and simple. He could also impale himself on one of the swords from his collection, but that would be messy, and he didn't know if he could do that. But either way, he would leave his family money. And he would leave them a note. He needed them to know that he truly loved them.

But he was tired. And he really wanted to die.

Heather's life was in turmoil. She stayed in her room now. And she watched a lot of TV. She had seen her father act out in anger and grab her mom violently by her arms and shake her in her chair. He had hit her, and her mom had slapped his face. She had heard the shouting and the screaming and the busting glass as vases crashed, and pictures fell from the walls. She withdrew from everything.

Heather's only solace resided in her sister.

Hope had made many new friends, and she had been training them up in the way they should go. She and her boyfriend had also been humping like rabbits.

The confusion and the eminent changes that were happening within her home-life allowed her more freedom to do as she pleased. She was glad her mom and dad were finally getting a divorce. Most of her friends' parents were already divorced. And they had been given more freedom, more money and more expensive gifts because of it.

She still wasn't going to like PJ. He was disgusting. But, he was strong, and he kept her mom occupied. She thought of him more as a trained monkey or a Seeing-Eye dog, and she looked forward to his sacrifice.

PJ was getting laid more than he had ever in his life. The girl at the Diner and the red head at the bar were both rocking his world. Tara was still acting very weird. But he had finally got to be with her again, too. All women were crazy bitches. He knew that. It all depended upon what you were willing to put up with and how good the pussy was.

Tara was going out of her mind. As her multiple personalities battled for control, she wasn't sleeping, she wasn't resting, and she had been blacking out consistently. She never knew what the next moment would bring. She couldn't remember the smallest of things; what day it was, where she was or how she had got there, what she had said or what she had been told she had done.

In Tara's mind, Tommy had become evil.

And Michael was suicidal. He was moving out. The county sheriff had served him with divorce papers.

And PJ …was exhibiting higher and higher prevalence and dominance in her life.

It never seemed to stop raining. To Tara, it meant that all of Heaven was crying.

She wasn't happy. She wasn't in love.

Sex with PJ was disappointing. She felt nothing. She trusted no one. And …her darkness was now …taking full control of her mind and spirit.

The darkness was defensive. It was manipulative and controlling. It was growing stronger. And it had an overwhelming desire …for a blood sacrifice.

Chapter Fifteen – The Blood of Jesus

"By the blood of Jesus Christ, our Lord and Savior, we are saved. Praise God. And …Hallelujah," The preacher man said excitedly. "And now, please open your Bibles and read along with me."

Tommy opened his bible and read along with the preacher, as he sat alone on the back row of the wooden pews. There were larger numbers of people in attendance this morning than he had anticipated. There were families dressed in their finest clothes, little girls in their fancy dresses and little boys with sullen faces pulling at their clip-on ties and their tightly buttoned shirts.

There were fussy children making noises, and there were babies crying. The church was filled with the sounds of life, and the joys of being alive.

"In the Old Testament, in Deuteronomy chapter eighteen, verses nine thru fourteen it is written," The preacher read out loud to the congregation. "Let no one be found among you who sacrifices their son or daughter in the fire, who practices divination or sorcery, interprets omens, engages in witchcraft, or casts spells, or who is a medium or spiritist or who consults the dead. Anyone who does these things is detestable to the LORD; because of these same detestable practices the LORD your God will drive out those nations before you. You must be blameless before the LORD your God. The nations you will dispossess, listen to those who practice sorcery or divination. But as for you, the LORD your God has not permitted you to do so."

"Now, please turn and read with me from the first book of John, chapter four, verses one through three," He continued. "Beloved, do not believe every spirit, but test the spirits to see whether they are from God, for many false prophets have gone out into the world. By this you know the Spirit of God: every spirit that confesses that Jesus Christ has come in the flesh is from God, and every spirit that does not confess Jesus is not from God. This is the spirit of the Antichrist, which you heard was coming and now is in the world already."

Tommy believed in Jesus Christ, and he had accepted him as his Lord and Savior when he was seven years old. His mom was a Baptist and his dad had been a Catholic.

At the time his parents were married, their union, because of their differences in faith, had been frowned upon. But their marriage had grown stronger in-spite of it, and he had been raised in the knowledge and teachings of the Christian faith.

He wasn't perfect. He knew he was a sinner. But he also knew that he was cleansed of his sins by the blood of Jesus. It didn't mean that he could do whatever he wanted and get away with it. It meant that his Father in Heaven loved him, and that he was forgiven.

He also believed that it was necessary for you to believe the Son of the Living God had died for you, and had risen again on the third day, but, you also had to follow Him, which meant, that you followed in His ways, and you were to learn from His teachings. And you were to have faith.

Tommy's mind began to wonder as the preacher gave his sermon. And he looked around the chapel room at the faces of the followers. He had once been with family here. He had once known all who had come. But now, they were all strangers to him.

He hadn't been to the morning church services here since he was a boy, back when he was only fourteen years old, since he had come here with Tara. He hadn't known why he had felt the need to come to church this morning; particularly, this church. But he felt he needed to find reason why Tara had come back into his life.

He hadn't spoken with her in days. He wondered why they had been brought back together, after all of these years. What was the purpose? What had been the reason?

Was he supposed to save her? What did the 'God of all Creation,' want him to do?

"Please stand and know that you are loved, and that you are wanted." The preacher said, bringing Tommy's attention back to the forefront. "All things are done according to God's plan and decision; and God chose us to be his own people in union with Christ because of his own purpose, based on what he had decided from the very beginning. You were chosen according to the purpose of God the Father and were made a holy people by his Spirit, to obey Jesus Christ and be purified by his blood. May grace and peace be yours in full measure."

As the preacher ended his sermon and dismissed the congregation, Tommy waited in the long line and shook his hand.

"Is this your first time visiting with us?" The preacher asked.

"No sir," Tommy answered. "I was a member here when I was a boy. I was baptized here, a long time ago."

"Welcome back." The preacher replied. "We hope to see you again. Please come back and join us whenever you can."

Tommy walked through the graveled parking lot to his car. It had gotten colder out, and the rain was still falling.

He fumbled with his keys for a moment as he searched for the right one, and then he sat down inside and started the engine.

He turned on the heat to defog the windows and he lit up a cigarette.

The rain came down in droves as he sat in his car and watched the members of the church pull out their umbrellas, run to their cars, and wait in lines with their headlights on to exit the parking lot. It was still early

Sunday morning, when the parking lot emptied and as others soon began arriving for the next service.

He heated his fingers by the warmth coming through the vents, and he thought about where he needed to go as he smoked. He was hungry. And he needed a friend, someone to talk to. So, he exited the graveled parking lot, and he turned his car towards Barstow. He was headed towards the Pancake Café. The girl he had met there was friendly, and she'd had a nice ass. He hadn't called her, though she'd given him her number. He hoped she was still working there, and that she remembered him.

The little restaurant was jam-packed as he pulled into the lot and searched for a place to park. The rain was still pouring down, as he walked briskly across the wet pavement, avoiding small pools of water, and opened the glass doors. As the bells jingled, Tommy was greeted by the waitress. She wasn't Allison, but she showed him to a freshly cleaned and open table booth. He shook off the rain and the cold, and he made himself comfortable.

As he began to eat his breakfast, two eggs over medium with bacon and toast, he sipped his coffee and he looked at his phone. There was nothing from Tara; no text messages and no calls, but he had received a message on social media.

Tommy's heart jumped, and he felt a large lump swell up in his throat. The message was from Rowan. The guy he had gone to school with, who had also been a drummer in

187

the band; the same guy, who had been convicted of murder.

"Who is this miserable prick that is making Tara's life so miserable?" Rowan's message read.

"I have no idea." Tommy replied. "I haven't heard from her in a while now. Her ex maybe? Her boyfriend?"

"The most recent post I got on 'Notifications' says it all. I assume it is her husband, or ex, He apparently has been victimizing our Tara for some time. I am just making inquiries." Rowan messaged. "As you well know, I have been 'out of the loop' for a while. Otherwise, she is pretty 'tight-lipped' about it."

"Well …," Tommy answered. "Her ex has a drinking problem. Her boyfriend has a 'stupid as a rock,' problem. So, it could be either one."

"Something has broken loose her tongue." Rowan continued. "My 'first love' is in distress …as I said, making inquiries. She is my true 'home-girl.' She lived just over the hill from our farm as I said, she was my first love."

"I'm finding that to be true of many of us." Tommy replied. "She was my first love, too."

"I loved her." Rowan messaged. "I loved her dad. I loved her mom. We were all close."

"I understand," Tommy texted. "Much sadness is hidden behind her pretty face and angelic smile."

"Indeed." Rowan stated. "I trust No one, yet there are things I must know. WE are a brotherhood. Any info that you can give me will be in confidence. Things might have to be done. Things that MUST be kept in confidence, comprehend?"

"I understand completely." Tommy replied. He didn't know where this conversation was leading, but he was already knee deep.

"I am not the man they have painted brother – I did not kill the girl I was convicted of murdering – yet I am a man who has become a 'thing' not to be trifled with. I have little left in this life to care about – but Tara? Tara? Tara I will always 'love' …and I 'like' little." Rowan related and continued. "Nothing on the internet is secure. Take down my number. From hence, that would be best – I must help her, even if she doesn't want it."

Tommy thought about the implications. Rowan was just speaking about murder. And by conversing with him on the subject matter, it made him an accomplice. He didn't want Rowan to have his number. And he wanted no part in murdering anyone either. So, he quickly searched for an application to download on-line, which would provide him with use of an alternate number to provide.

"This is my number," Tommy texted Rowan's phone.

"Got it," He replied. "Something needs to be done and done quickly. Someone needs to 'disappear.' And I have the means to do it. I have nothing else to lose."

Tommy suddenly remembered a conversation he'd had with Tara. She had told him that Rowan did not remember him.

"By the way, I didn't think you'd remember me," Tommy texted.

"Of course, I do, you held your own as a drummer after we all graduated, and I heard you became very good." Rowan answered. "I have to go for now. But if you learn anything, or know anything that would help 'our purpose,' let me know. You can always reach me here."

"Understood," Tommy replied.

Tommy put down his phone. He finished his breakfast, which had already grown cold. And he sat in silence as he drank the last drop of his coffee. He had wanted to interview Rowan about the crimes he was convicted of, but he would never have thought he would be conversing with him regarding murdering someone. He quickly gathered his composure and got up from the table booth.

He wished he had seen Allison again, but his conversation with Rowan would have thrown him off his game, so, in another way he was relieved he hadn't. He would try to see her another time.

He paid his check, and he ran out hurriedly to his car through the rain.

He could barely find his key or see the keyhole for the blinding rain and the water pouring heavily into his eyes.

He looked up for a brief moment, and he felt the rush of falling rain hitting upon his face. It was refreshing. He felt inexplicably alive.

And then suddenly, he felt an agonizing …and excruciating pain.

He saw a white light.

And then …his entire world …went dark.

Chapter Sixteen – Refraction's of Light

The large, recessed windows, with their custom curtains drawn back, displayed the reflections and refractions of the small-city lights upon the windows' glass. The walls of the petite square room were plain and painted an egg-shell colored white, although it looked somewhat darker, since the room's lights had been dimmed. There were black metal boxes on tall silver poles with red, yellow and green buttons, and with slowly moving arrays of lights in the middle. They were beeping. And the bed frame he had awakened in …had rails.

He was cold. And then, he realized …that he could not move. He was handcuffed to the bed rails.

"Everything is alright, Mr. MacAnully." A calming voice said as Tommy tried to focus his eyes and come to full consciousness. "We need you to relax and remain calm. Everything is okay, and everything is going to be alright."

"Where am I?" Tommy mumbled. "What happened?"

"You've been asleep for a few days now." The nurse answered. "We've been told you had been in an accident. And there were signs of some very strong narcotics in your system." She continued. "The drugs may have saved your life. You are in Crittenden County Hospital. My name is Sheila. I'm the head floor nurse. And we're glad you made it back."

"Am I all in one piece?" Tommy asked. He could feel his legs and feet, and he could move them slightly. But he was restrained, and he wasn't fully cognizant of his body's mobility or of his surroundings. "And why am I tied down?"

The nurse motioned toward the opened doorway, and to the two Kentucky State Police Officers who were standing guard by the wall.

"The State Police Detective has been notified that you have awakened." She said. "It's currently two-twenty-four in the morning. He'll be able to answer any questions you may have when he arrives in a few hours."

Tommy sighed deeply.

Nurse Sheila fluffed his pillows and made him swallow his pills.

"Now, lay back and get some rest." She said. "I'll be back to check on you in a couple of hours."

Tommy couldn't help it. He closed his eyes. And he went to sleep.

In what seemed like seconds later, Tommy awakened with a fright. The lights were on, and the windows shades were still pulled wide open, and the sun was blinding.

He was surrounded by people in uniforms.
He attempted to focus his eyes.

"Mr. MacAnully, I am Detective Hawkins from the Kentucky State Police Department." The Detective stated. "Can you tell me the last thing you remember?"

Tommy was still trying to focus, his head hurt profusely, and his memory was very cloudy, foggy and he was confused.

"I remember getting something to eat." Tommy replied. "And I remember it was raining." He continued. "Can you tell me why I am tied down? Was I in an accident? Have I had a back injury?"

"No sir." Detective Hawkins stated. "You have a concussion and you've been found to have a high concentration of a previously unknown narcotic in your blood stream." He continued. "Can you tell me about your relationship with Mrs. Tara Rozanski, and with her husband, a Mr. Michael Rozanski? When was the last time you saw them?"

"What? Why?" Tommy asked. "Has something happened to Tara? Oh my God, is she okay?"

"When was the last time you saw her? And when was the last time you were at her house, Mr. MacAnully?" Detective Hawkins asked. "When was the last time you were inside?"

"What's happening?" Tommy asked as he tried his strength against the restraints. "Am I under arrest or something?"

The detective began to speak openly and related knowledge of Tommy's life. He knew the names of his family and friends, and he had researched and documented his whereabouts over the last several years.

He spoke of Tommy's traffic tickets in Pennsylvania, his loss of jobs and of his court appearances, including his divorce and child custody agreements in the late nineties.

"Mr. MacAnully," The Detective said. "You were found covered in blood. The blood was that of Mr. Michael Rozanski." The Detective paused.

"Oh my God." Tommy exclaimed. "Is Michael okay? What happened?"

"Mr. MacAnully, you are under arrest for the murder of Michael Rozanski in the first degree. You are being charged with Conspiracy to Commit Murder in the first degree. You are being charged with Unlawful Trespassing and Breaking and Entering. You are also being charged with Terroristic Threatening, Possession and the Use of Illegal Drugs over Five Ounces, Possession of an Unregistered Firearm, fourteen counts of Rape and Sodomy of minor female children under the ages of twelve and fifteen-years-old and you are being charged for the Possession and the Making as well as the possible distribution of Child Pornography."

The Detective pulled out his Miranda card and began to read out loud.

"You have the Right to remain silent. Anything you say can and will be used against you in a Court of Law. You have the Right to an Attorney before making a statement. And you may have your Attorney with you during questioning." Detective Hawkins read. "If you cannot afford an Attorney and desire one, the Court will appoint one for you. You may stop the questioning at any time by refusing to answer further or by requesting to consult with your Attorney."

Tommy listened and tried to understand why this was happening.

"Do you understand each of these rights as I have explained them to you?" Detective Hawkins asked.

Tommy nodded yes.

"With these rights in mind," Detective Hawkins continued. "Do you wish to talk to us now?"

"I want a lawyer." Tommy replied.

Chapter Seventeen – Scene of the Crime

The crime scene was horrific. There was blood everywhere. The police officers had marked off the areas outside and within the house with yellow tape that read: POLICE INVESTIGATION DO NOT CROSS.

"We found the body upstairs." Detective Hawkins said. "His hands were tied behind his back, and he was hanging by the neck from a scarf attached to the closet doorknob with a Medieval Sword penetrating through his abdomen and exiting through his torso to the right of his lower spine. The coroner is determining whether or not he died from strangulation or the stab wound."

The Police Sergeant covered her mouth and nose with a handkerchief as she reviewed the panoramic view of the living room and the adjoining hallway and staircase.

"We have the suspect in custody." Detective Hawkins continued. "And we are still collecting evidence to support the current charges and in the investigation of the assailants past."

The body of Michael Rozanski had been taken to the County Coroner's Office. The scarf he had been hanged from, was left as it was found, dangling ominously from the doorknob. And the sword was stood up in the corner.

The victim had bled out on the floor. Boot prints, that had been tracked through the blood, could be found throughout the small alcove, down the steps, across the

199

living room and out unto the driveway. Blood stains, smudges and handprints were highly visible along the staircase railing and the adjacent yellow-beige colored walls. It was surreal, grotesque, and the air was morbid.

"Do we have sworn statements from the victim's wife?" Sergeant Cavanaugh asked as she followed Detective Hawkins up the staircase and swept the scene and the blood splatter with her trained eyes. "Was she in the home when the murder occurred? Did the victim have life insurance and could his wife be implicated?"

"She was not." Detective Hawkins stated. "We have sworn affidavits confirming her and her children's whereabouts on the night and the subsequent nights following her husband's death." He continued. "Her next-door neighbor, Mr. Millard Jones has also testified and given sworn statements to this fact. The body of Mr. Rozanski wasn't discovered until a few days after the murder had occurred. The coroner is currently determining the exact time of his death."

The Detective came to a halt as the Sergeant entered the bedroom.

"This I needed to show you." He said as he pointed to the blood-stained floor. "It's not something easily believed or conveyed."

The Sergeant viewed the hardwood floor of the victim's bedroom, and she gasped.

In front of the closet door, where the victim's body was found hanging from the doorknob, a large pentagram was drawn out upon the hardwood floor …in blood.

"I assume this is the victims' blood." The Sergeant stated questioningly as she continued to hold the handkerchief over her mouth and nose. "Have DNA samples been taken?"

"They have." The Detective answered. "They have been sent for analysis. We don't have the equipment or capabilities locally, so, it could take several weeks for the results to be determined."

"What else have you found?" The Sergeant asked.

"The victim knew the assailant, and there were no signs of forced entry. A Samsung cell phone was found in the circle beneath the body." Detective Hawkins stated. "It was unlocked. It belonged to the suspect in custody, and it had the victims' blood as well as the suspect's fingerprints on it."

"Did you get the proper warrants and search and seizure paperwork needed?" She asked. "It sounds like an open and shut case as long as we don't take any shortcuts. This has already begun making the regional news, and it will probably go national. My office has been notified by the Federal Bureau of Investigation, outlining our need for their assistance."

"Does he have any priors?" Sergeant Cavanaugh continued. "And, other than the obvious occultist references, have we determined a motive."

"Murder is congruent with a crime of passion." Hawkins replied. "He and Mrs. Rozanski had known one another since grade school. According to Mrs. Rozanski, he had an obsessive-compulsive personality that bordered on the sociopathic. He had been stalking her for years." The detective continued. "We are researching his banking history and travel logs, airline ticket purchases, traffic tickets, receipts, and phone and credit card records to determine if there is a pattern. We have uncovered evidence of his whereabouts in Pennsylvania during the time Mrs. Rozanski was living there. And we are researching unsolved cold cases during that timeframe." He continued. "Also, Mrs. Rozanski has provided video evidence of Mr. MacAnully driving past her property on multiple occasions and has stated that she had witnessed his behavior escalating over the last few months, including his coming to her property with loaded handguns and threatening her verbally. Further, she stated he has a Narcissistic personality, and she believes traumatic events have caused him to develop a dissociative identity disorder."

"Why hadn't she contacted the police previously?" Sergeant Cavanaugh asked.

"He had no prior criminal history on record. Mrs. Rozanski stated she had known him for years, and she is one of those people with a psychological degree who believes they can change the world." Detective Hawkins answered. "She was unaware that his obsessive behavior could escalate into physical altercations or homicide."

The Detective and the Sergeant descended the staircase and stood in Rozanski's living room, where a glowing white lit ornament of a small moon sat on display in the middle of a large mahogany entertainment center.

"It's highly probable," the Detective continued. "That this isn't his only murder victim." He paused. "He may have been murdering people for many years. The significance of the victim being hung by a doorknob suggests his being a part of the Cobal religion. This ritual is used as a symbol to all those who attempt to expose the group's current perceptions by the mainstream. Also, the sword is very reminiscent of a murder committed twenty or so years ago in a toy soldier museum."

"We need to get a psychological evaluation of the suspect completed right away." Sergeant Cavanaugh suggested. "He needs to be found competent enough to stand trial."

"Agreed," Detective Hawkins stated. "We have him currently on suicide watch." He paused. "We definitely have motive for murder, and the pictorial evidence on the subject's phone indicates that he is also a child predator. Also, once we are given further light on the circumstances regarding his whereabouts and correlations to other crime victims …we may very well have a serial killer on our hands."

Chapter Eighteen – Delusional Obsession

It was raining. It seemed to always be raining. The dark grey skies covered the world and blanketed the light. It was getting colder as the seasons began to change. It was also getting darker. And it was becoming more and more rare to see the sun.

All she could do was cry. Her husband was dead. He had been murdered. She would never see him again, talk with him again or touch him again. Her girls were devastated.

Their father, their dad had been murdered in their own home. Their lives would never be the same. There was a sense of extreme violation, remorse, betrayal and brutality that was causing her to shut down and try not to feel. But she had to be strong. Her children needed her.

Tara sat outside on her mother's back porch and stared out into the rain. She couldn't think clearly. So much had happened in such a short amount of time.

"Why had Tommy done this?" She asked herself over and over in her mind. "What had she done to him in the past to make him act out with such malice and such violence?"

She hadn't seen her husband's body, until he had been taken to the County Morgue. When she and her girls had arrived home after visiting with her mom that weekend, they had seen the blood and the handprints on the wall.

She had called the police right away. And she had waited for them to arrive.

The police had questioned her. And she had told them everything that she knew. She hadn't known who could have killed her husband, until the fingerprints had been analyzed and Tommy had been taken into custody. He had been found unconscious, sitting in his car with the engine running, in the Marion Springs Kroger store parking lot.

And, she had been told that he was covered in blood.

The police Detective had asked her invasive questions, mostly about her relationship with Tommy and of her relationship with Michael. And she had told them the truth. She and her husband were working through their marital problems, after filing for divorce, and they had begun to be a family again.

And, as for Tommy, he was only a friend. Someone she normally would help. He was not the kind of person she would date. Besides, she was a married woman. Tommy was obsessive and borderline sociopathic. He had a narcissistic personality, and now, with the recent escalation of events, he had become a violent, psychotic murderer.

She had known Tommy since grade school. But there had never been anything between them. They had been friends, but she had been friends with many people. She had never even kissed him, ever. They hadn't even spoken much. He had texted her frequently, but she had never answered him. She didn't feel it was the right thing to do since she was a married woman.

She had informed the Detective that she had video surveillance of Tommy passing by her house on numerous occasions and she had provided that evidence to the detective. He had also pounded on her door one morning in a panic, brandishing two loaded handguns. And she provided copies of his delusional text messages.

They would prove his obsessive and compulsive nature, in which he had expressed his undying love for her.

She never thought it would end up like this.

Suddenly, memories began to flood her mind.

Tommy had been there, and he had witnessed Dan when he was molesting her in the church in Michigan. And he had done nothing to help her. She recalled seeing his eyes through the window glass as she was being raped. He had been watching.

He had also told her that he would tell everyone that she was a slut and a whore, right after he had pledged his love to her.

And, he had been the cause of Dan's violent response towards her that very same afternoon.

More memories raced into her mind. Tommy had been the one who had dropped her off in the Kroger store parking lot, the night Dan had dragged her from the car, and had violently raped her again, and had almost strangled her to death; the same night as the car accident that had left her paralyzed.

"Tommy was present at every tragedy in my life." Tara thought to herself. "Oh my God. He'd been watching me. He'd been orchestrating everything."

Tara paused.

"Could Tommy have also run our car off the road that night?" Tara contemplated. "He was there when it happened. He had pulled glass from my face and my hands. Oh my God. Oh my God."

All Tara could do …was cry.

Chapter Nineteen – One Way Mirror

The room itself was a cliché. It was small with painted gray walls. A rectangular table sat in the middle with two hard wooden chairs on either side. There were no windows. There were no decorative markings. There was only a large mirror at one end, the kind you'd see in the movies; a one-way mirror where people from an otherwise hidden room could peer in.

Tommy sat at the table facing the mirror. He was donned in an orange jumpsuit. He was barefoot, and his hands and feet were chained together, in such a way as to only allow him a shuffled walk.

He had undergone intense psychiatric evaluations and testing. He had been asked every question imaginable from: "What does this ink blot look like on this piece of paper?" to: "Have you ever been molested? Do you have fantasies about little girls? Does killing someone excite you?" He was exhausted.

The Psychiatric Police Examiner, Hilbert Brody, and Sergeant Cavanaugh stood on the other side of the mirror.

"What's your evaluation of the suspect in custody?" Cavanaugh asked.

"Based upon my questioning and the evidence we have on file in his case," Brody stated. "I don't believe we'll go to trial. The suspect is highly delusional. He has

211

created his own world, a fantasy, and he believes what he's saying is true. That's why he passed the polygraph."

"So, you believe he'll be institutionalized?" Cavanaugh replied.

"My understanding is this." Brody continued. "He believes that he and Mrs. Rozanski were lovers and that they had been for some time, yet this is emphatically denied by Mrs. Rozanski. He further states that they had been communicating via text messaging for months, however, according to his own personal phone records, he was the only one communicating. There are no return text messages from Mrs. Rozanski to substantiate his claim."

Brody paused and then began again. "Furthermore, we have interviewed the witnesses to his defense, a Mr. Sarge M. Ball and a Mr. Seth P. King. They have related the story Mr. MacAnully has stated on record, but it is only hearsay. They have only repeated the story he related. With the exception of Mr. Ball's account of assisting Mrs. Rozanski with her HVAC system, they have nothing tangible that would hold up in a court of law."

"We are still attempting to locate a Ms. Meghan Johnson, but she doesn't seem to exist, or at least, there is no evidence currently of her U.S. citizenship." Cavanaugh stated. "It's possible, since all contact was made via social media, that a false identity was produced."

"My point exactly." Brody answered. "My belief is that Mr. MacAnully has created his own world, his own reality, and he's attempted to pull other viable cohorts and friends into his psychotic illusion." Brody continued. "Mr. MacAnully has developed a Dissociative Personality Disorder, more commonly known as a split personality disorder. And at least one of his personalities is sociopathic with evident homicidal tendencies."

"We have investigated the area near the victims' home." Cavanaugh stated. "Detective Hawkins reported the area was as Mr. MacAnully had stated and as substantiated by his friend Mr. Ball, however, given the amount of time Mr. MacAnully had invested in stalking Mrs. Rozanski, he could have easily created the scene himself to make it seem more plausible." Cavanaugh continued. "We also believe he had been watching her property from the woods across the street from her for a very long time."

"Have we been able to tie the suspect to any other unsolved crimes?" Brody asked. "His specific disorder was most likely developed in his early teen years. This could be something that has been a repeated cycle of events over the course of his lifetime."

"We're still attempting to draw a correlation between any accidental deaths and homicides that occurred within one degree of separation from Mrs. Rozanski." Cavanaugh stated. "It's like finding a needle in a haystack. It might close a few cold cases and bring closure to victims' families, but it's hard to find evidence of crimes labeled accidental or those that were closed because of death listed as by suicide."

Just then, they heard the suspect shout out loudly behind the mirrored glass.

"I am not a murderer!" Tommy screamed. "I didn't kill anybody, and I am not a pedophile or a rapist!"

The Sergeant and the Psychiatric Examiner exited the room.

Chapter Twenty – Reasonable Insanity

The Crittenden County Courthouse was an historic work of architecture designed by a high-ranking French mason in the early eighteen hundreds. The beautiful arched windows of painted glass were accented by its large columns, and high reaching towers that were reminiscent of early European castles. It sat in the heart of the county seat with its roadways circling counterclockwise around it. It held the pulse of a modern-day city, with an old city feel and charm.

They met behind closed doors in the Judge's chambers. The attorneys for both the prosecution and the defense had waived jurisprudence, bringing the suspect to judicial trial based upon the diagnosis provided to the court, by the Psychiatric Police Examiner. His diagnosis was further substantiated by a separate psychological evaluation, conducted by an unbiased third party. In either case however, the Attorney for the defense was prepared to plead his client not guilty by reason of insanity.

Court ordered pre-trial mental examinations occur as the result of two distinct legal concepts: one, that some defendants are of such a mental condition at the time of the alleged crime that they should not be held responsible for acts which would otherwise be criminal – the insanity defense; and two, that some defendants are of such a mental condition that they cannot meaningfully participate in their defense and that it would be unfair to try such people – incompetency to stand trial. Legal insanity is usually phased in terms of the defendant's inability to understand the nature and consequences of his act, or if he did understand it, his inability to understand right from wrong with reference to it.

Theoretically, legal insanity negates the issues of guilt or responsibility.

"We have the eyes and ears of the entire country upon us gentlemen." Judge Watts stated. "The local and national news agencies are broadcasting live media coverage of our every waking move in this case. I won't have this turned into a media circus, especially this close to my re-election campaign."

"Your Honor, the prosecution formally agrees to forgo charges against the accused until such time as he is found to be competent to stand trial." Attorney Johnson stated.

"And, your Honor, the defense agrees to waive the client's Fifth Amendment rights and plead no contest to the charges until such time as the defendant is deemed competent to stand trial as well." Attorney Collins stated for the defense. "Provided the defendant is not formally sentenced to a prison facility and will also not be subject to harsher punishment up to and including the death penalty."

"Gentlemen, if this is agreed upon by the Prosecution for the State and the Attorney for the Defense, then we can count this matter closed." Judge Watts agreed. "The accused will be held in the Crittenden County Mental

Institution Facility for a period no less than twenty years, or until such time as he is found to be competent enough to stand trial for the crimes he has been charged with." Judge Watts continued as he slammed his gavel. "Please join me this afternoon. I want you both to be present. I'll have my people contact the media and call for a Press Conference. I'll have it set up after lunch. And then, gentlemen, we can all go back to our normal lives."

The Press gathered on the Courthouse lawn that afternoon, as Tommy was escorted from his six by five jail cell into a black, unmarked and bulletproof vehicle.

The Judge read his statement to the media as the cameras flashed and as Tommy was led through the metal detectors, past the armed guards and entered the foyer of the Crittenden County Mental Institutional Facility.

As the Press Conference drew to a close, and LIVE News feeds of the verdict and the sentencing of the accused were being broadcast all across the continental United States and Canada, Tommy was forcefully injected with a strong sedative, to keep him calm and complacent, as he was fitted into a straight-jacket and placed inside his new home with padded walls.

Everything had happened so fast. Whether it was because of the drugs in his system, the environment he was thrown into or the reality to which he was presented, whatever the reason, Tommy's brain simply began to shut down.

The enormity and magnitude of the situation, as well as the complexity of the events that had transpired, was completely overwhelming. He was lost. He was alone.

And he began to doubt his own sanity.

Chapter Twenty-One – The Seclusion Room

The seclusion room is especially designed for detainees with violent and challenging behavior who can potentially cause harm to themselves or to those who are charged with their care. Psychiatric Institutions are legally allowed to confine an individual who exhibits such conduct in isolation for a period of up to twenty-four hours. After this timeframe, paperwork must be documented and re-signed by the Chief Administrator of the medical facility, in order to further a patient's term in said confinement.

The walls were padded. The color of the room was beige. And no sound could be heard from outside. There were also no windows. It was impossible to determine the time of day, other than by the small screen television set mounted in the uppermost corner to the left, facing the door. The set was tuned and locked onto the Kentucky Educational Television Network channel, but it at least provided him with a small window into the outside world.

Tommy had a long time to think things through. To the best of his knowledge, he had been incarcerated in this facility for sixty days, coupled with his time in the hospital and the local jail; he estimated he had now lost four months, two weeks and five days of his life.

He wasn't allowed to communicate with anyone using the internet or telecommunications, because he wasn't allowed access. But he could send and receive letters via the U.S. Postal Service, though, all written correspondence was thoroughly screened by the administration staff, and he was never completely sure if what he had sent was actually being mailed or if what he had received, was everything that had been delivered.

He was allowed to have visitors, but no more than three at one time. And those who visited with him had to allow a search of their person, to ensure that no drug paraphernalia, communications devices or weapons were being smuggled in. Seth and his wife Sienna had visited him, as had Sarge and a few others. It hurt him deeply when his parents visited, because no parent wants to see their child in such a place after being accused of such heinous crimes.

"Remember," Tommy's mom said. "The Apostle Paul spent much of his life and ministry in prison. God has always had a purpose for your life, my son. And never forget that we love you, and we will love you forever."

His friends Seth and Sarge both tried to give him hope and help him remain positive. After all they had been through together, regarding the events leading up to his incarceration, they had no solid evidence to provide that would remotely help him undo the physical evidence and charges that had been levied against him.

He also had a psychological diagnosis stating that he was incompetent to withstand trial. It meant the State believed he was mentally incapable.

People who suffer from mental illness are marginalized and sane people tend to keep them at bay. Everyone believes they are crazy and dangerous because of their condition. They often suffer from nightmares because of the chemically induced straight-jackets, and they often awaken violently when they become aware of their dreams.

"We're killing off our prophets." Tommy thought to himself. "And we're drugging our truest believers."

After analyzing his thoughts, he decided that he must truly be insane.

BOOM. BOOM. BOOM. BOOM. The sounds resounded upon his door.

"Mr. MacAnully, you have a visitor." The staff member shouted through the small vent in the door. "Make yourself presentable. I'll bring you a change of clothing, and I'll take you to the visitation room shortly."

Tommy hadn't had a visitor in over a month, and he had been suffering from major depression. He was seldom allowed to bathe of his own accord, and he smelled of urine. He was in no shape or condition to entertain visitors.

He was escorted to the showers a few minutes later, and he was hosed off like cattle in a barn. There was no privacy. He had no control. He was treated humanely, though most of his human rights had been stricken from him. He was given clean clothing and then his wrists and ankles were bound with Leathers.

Leathers are a four-point cuff system. They are called leathers because they've traditionally been made of leather; it makes them harder to bite through and almost impossible to get out of.

He was led into a little room with large one-inch-thick Plexiglas windows so that everything could be seen from the outside. It had a rectangular table and two uncomfortably hard wooden chairs.

Two staff guards stood outside the door while he waited alone in the room. And then, suddenly, he became aware that his visitor was approaching. He could see her glide through the opened lobby and wheel herself through the doors held open by the staff guards.

As she rolled up to the table across from him in her wheelchair, he struggled for words, but he found none.

She was as beautiful as ever and her smile almost made him forget where he was.

"Every once in a while," Tara stated after she made herself comfortable with her surroundings, "when the drugs don't work and I'm awake, weeping and praying to understand why …one thing always comes to me with inconsolable crystalline clarity …what you did to me was inexcusable and will hurt me until the day I die. Why did you attack me, not only in the most vulnerable and fragile time in my life but, at all? How could I have possibly deserved that?"

Tommy sat silently and listened. He didn't have the words to answer.

"Do you know that all you did was destroy my faith in people? All people." Tara continued. "What little shred that I was still clawing to hold onto, you took that from me. I'm not the same person anymore. I don't trust anybody anymore. I don't love anybody anymore."

Tommy sat across the table, looking at this person who was speaking to him, feeling like he was trapped in a conversation that she had been having with him in her mind for months; a conversation he had not been a part of.

"Somewhere in me I just need to know what I did years ago that warranted an attack on my soul that was so vengeful and contrived." Tara continued. "One thing that stuck with me of all the things that you said was that you wanted to keep me honorable. And all that does is make me think of being a scared fourteen-year-old kid who got way in over her head, but even so, a fourteen-year-old kid who wrote letter upon letter begging Dan to leave me alone because I never wanted to have sex with him. I never did. I couldn't go to my mother." Tara said and then paused for a moment. "Until the day she died, my mom thought I was a whore. There was no discussing that time in my life in any way that would have ended with her granting me forgiveness for it. It doesn't matter who pushed whose way into whose room. It doesn't matter who pushed himself inside me while I cried and begged him to stop. It doesn't matter that I sat in my bathroom with my feet bouncing up and down reflexively on cold tile while the blood dripped, dripped, dripped into the toilet bowl. And it didn't matter that no amount of Tylenol was going to make it hurt any less. In any way, in her mind, it was always going to be my fault."

Tommy knew there was nothing he could say. She had not come to visit him to find answers. She had come to resolve herself of all guilt.

"So, I guess my shot at being honorable disappeared when I was fourteen. And then, here I am now, and according to you, I guess I'm still not honorable." Tara stated. "I haven't managed to regain even a bit of it, according to you." Tara paused again and then leaned in closer. "But I can't figure out for the life of me when God made you the keeper of my honor and my respectability and my decency and goodness. But I am forever sorry that I failed you."

During Tara's rant of thoughts without questions, Tommy realized that not once had she brought up the murder of her husband. Not once had she taken any responsibility for her actions. It was the same as the night they had been together, and she had confessed her sins.

But, she hadn't confessed her sins. She had confessed the sins of others.

She was playing a record over and over in her mind, as she must have done consistently over these past several months. She was caught up in incidents that had occurred outside of the realm of his control or understanding. And even in her mind, her own thoughts conveyed her lies.

Tap. Tap. Tap. Resounded on the Plexiglas, signaling the time limit for the visitation was ten minutes before conclusion.

"From the time I was fourteen," Tara continued. "I heard this voice telling me every day that I was ugly and shameful and fat and disgusting and a whore and a slut and useless and I didn't have a voice to counter that. Not my mom. Not my friends. Certainly not him. He ran with his tail tucked between his legs to Georgia and took over a mega church and left me here to deal with it all on my own." She stated. "And I spent time with every boy I could find who would make me feel just a little bit better about myself just for a little bit of time. Somebody that would tell me I was pretty and good. Somebody who might see my heart. Dust it off a little bit and see that I was viable and strong and, yes, filled with maybe not honor but something close maybe. But it never worked for very long. And I just felt worse every time. And then one day I started hearing this inner voice. Really, really quiet at first but then louder and louder and it was a voice telling me that I was beautiful and worth something and that I had something to bring. And I started listening to that voice. That voice made me a really good wife and mother. That voice helped me quiet an alcoholic's demons for over ten years. That voice kept me going

229

every day when the other voice told me to lay down and die. Every time I wanted to just lay there, that voice would say to get up, get up, get up."

Tommy listened in tentatively.

"And so, I did." Tara continued. "And then the alcoholic's demons got the better of him. And the bruises were harder to hide. And the voice got too fucking loud. And so, I took a chance and went to a reunion of people who were supposed to be my friends and care about me. And then, you set PJ up. And indirectly, you set me up. When she sent him those pictures, and he asked her for additional pictures – yes, yes he did – it all came rushing back. Just how ugly and useless and unattractive and worthless and stupid and fat and homely that I truly was. That I was so fucking ugly that he had to look at her on a phone screen when he had me right there in front of him and that he couldn't see my heart over her bare-naked ass." Tara paused. "Just for one day. One day it took to figure out that you were controlling the bare-naked ass, but the damage was done. And the weirdest thing happened that day. The other voice? The good one? It went away."

Tara pushed herself away from the table and turned towards the door.

"It went away." She continued. "It's never come back. I don't think it ever will. You took that too. Will you ever grasp what you've done?"

Tara smiled at Tommy cruelly. "Sex with PJ is great, by the way. I want to make sure you know that." She said to hurt Tommy deeply. "I don't know if we'd be together if it wasn't for you. We became 'us' because of you. He has since moved into Michael's old room upstairs."

"You deserve one another." Tommy replied. "And you can keep hating me if that makes you feel better. Keep trying to hurt me if that makes you feel good. I refuse to hate you in return. I will love you in spite of the anger and in spite of the hatred. I did not kill Michael. I am a sinner, but I am not the evil monster you have created me out to be."

"You're exactly as evil as I believe you to be." Tara replied. "You're just a better liar than I gave you credit for. And you are delusional."

As Tommy's daily allotment of medically prescribed drug treatments began to wear off, his focus became clearer, and he was able to put aside his love for Tara and concentrate on his current state of events and the situations at hand.

"Tara, you are fucking crazy. You need to seek professional help." Tommy stated. "I didn't kill Michael and I think you know that. And are you seriously telling me that I forced you and PJ together?" Tommy paused. "Are you saying I raped you with another man's dick? Damn it! You are out of your fucking mind! You waited ten years to have sex and you chose a Neanderthal? He's a fucking trained dog; a chimpanzee in fucking overall's." Tommy said as he rose up out of his chair causing the guards to come into the room.

"The darkness inside of you is what killed your husband. You set me up. You fucking played me like a fool!" Tommy shouted. "You framed me for a murder that I did not commit and somehow, I haven't figured everything out yet, but you also framed me for the child rape and pornography charges. You've been doing this to men for years, haven't you? You've been killing people all of your life, haven't you Tara?" Tommy shouted.

Instantly, as Tommy's outbursts became more belligerent and outwardly violent, an alarm sounded and several additional staff members came running into the room, and they quickly held him back down in his chair and administered a fast-acting sedative.

Tommy went numb.

Then, the staff guards apologized to Tara for their patients' behavior, and they held open the glass doors for her ease of way out of the room.

Tara paused as she watched his struggle, and then she wheeled herself over beside him, and she kissed Tommy one last time on his cheek.

"By the way," she whispered. "You don't have to worry about Rowan anymore. I guess, in a way, you don't have to worry about anything anymore."

Tara smiled nonchalantly. And then her smile turned cruel.

"Rowan died soon after you were arrested. It was self-inflicted. The first boy who ever saw me as beautiful, committed suicide, and I blame you for that too." Tara stated glaringly. "Oh, and the church fires …they still rage in Georgia. Another of Dan's churches has caught flame; Church two-thirteen. Isn't it funny how the real monsters of this world walk in the light?" She said as she touched his hand. "And the darkness …it seems to consume us all."

A moment of calm as Tara wheeled herself away through the opened doors, and as a staff nurse wiped the drool from Tommy's chin. And a verse from the Book of Mathew came into his mind.

"For what will it profit a man if he gains the whole world and forfeits his soul? Or what shall a man give in return for his soul?"

Soon thereafter, he found himself being wheeled down the hallway in a wheelchair much like Tara's, to his room.

"Love will fuck you up, more than drugs ever will." Tommy screamed out in his mind. He couldn't move. He was trapped in a chemically induced straight-jacket.

And then, he heard the cold metal steel-on-steel sound, as the staff nurse left him alone in his padded jail cell and slammed and locked the heavy metal door behind him.

Tommy's memories would return to him in shrouded veils and flashes of emotion, but it would be years before he would place the pieces together in his mind.

Over the loudspeakers, the TV, or quite possibly in his mind, a familiar song began to play. He recognized it. It was Alice Cooper, Poison.

♫ "Your cruel device. Your blood like ice. One look could kill. My pain, your thrill. I wanna love you but I better not touch. I wanna hold you, but my senses tell me to stop. I wanna kiss you, but I want it too much. I wanna taste you, but your lips are venomous poison. You're poison runnin' through my veins. You're poison; I don't wanna break these chains." ♫

And the music filled the quiet and the void …and the darkness in the light.

Chapter Twenty-Two – The Darkness in the Light

The darkness was all consuming. It encompassed the moon and the stars and the waters and the air. It moved upon the waters of the earth, and it called unto itself the unnatural creatures that guarded the shadows; they were the deceivers of truth that danced between myth, reality and legend.

The un-holy beings were servants of the darkness; they guarded her sanctuary; she could see through their eyes, and they awaited upon their master's call.

In Native American folklore, the legends of these creatures are transmitted by oral tradition. Only a witch can make a Rougarou, a skin-walker, either by turning into a wolf herself, or by cursing others with Lycanthropy. They are the guardians of the Old Ways.

Their race was created centuries ago when the Old Religion was new. And they have been drawn to the magic and the darkness of their creators ever since.

The beasts of the wood would be released upon the world at the coming of the new millennia, at the end of the age of men, but until then, they bred, and they howled, and they grunted outside the fires light as the flames grew higher and higher unto starlit skies.

"As it was in the beginning," The Coven chanted in unison. "So, shall it be in the end."

In the ways of the Old Religion, the twelve in robes gathered together within the sacred circle, and they celebrated the divine polarity and union of the gods and goddesses. Their Tribe, their Coven, required a sworn oath of secrecy. Those who stepped within the ritual circle could not disclose the names or the happenings.

They found tranquility and freedom in their union of souls, as they danced around the fire that raged beneath the darkened moon.

"Love is the law and love is the bond." Hope professed as she led the circle. "Come to the circle with love in your heart and be free of judgment."

It was the night of spiritual awakening. It was a time of new beginnings. On this beautiful night with the full moon shining brightly, they would draw down the moon and the high priestess would speak the words of the goddess. And those who had gathered together in the circle would experience profound belonging, as they released their inhibitions into the wind.

Tonight, Hope would be acknowledged by her Coven mothers and sisters, as the youngest High Priestess to attain the honor within their congregation. The Coven recognized her commitment, loyalty, and her expansion of their old ways, their Old Religion.

The Coven also came to honor the creative forces of the universe. The energy, harmony and divinity of sexual polarity between goddess and gods, and they emphasized their importance as part of their religious practice, as it was in the ancient days.

"Before we are ...before we were," Hope stated. "Before our ancestors could be called human, then did it begin, and through the ages untold have the Old Ways shaped humanity and were part of the very creation of our race."

The Coven is a place to belong. Humans have always had a need for a sense of belonging to a clan, tribe, or village. A place to belong is one of the most important needs of the spirit.

The concept of sin is not part of the ways of the Old Religion. The attitudes and practices concerning sin, shame, sex and other moral issues create a fundamental division between paganism and the conventional Christian culture. They do not feel shame for their bodies or for themselves. They understand that they were created in love and beauty and do not accept the psychotic belief in original sin, for which they must be forgiven or saved. There is a reason for the end of the age.

There are currently more Americans who identify as practicing Witches than there are members of the Presbyterian faith. Wicca re-branded the term witchcraft for the new millennial culture. The terms Witch and Pagan no longer mean satanic or demonic. Wicca is now known as a pre-Christian tradition that promotes free thought and understanding of earth and nature.

The Old Religion began thirty-five-thousand years ago and they worshiped the goddess of nature. Their societies were egalitarian and focused on the female, not the male.

Then the invaders swept in, and they were followed by Christianity whose secular authorities began a four-hundred-year campaign to kill the Old Religion.

"The Christians cannot tell us how to worship." Hope said. "They cannot tell us how to connect with the divine. That is between the angels and our inner selves. And they cannot tell us how to pray."

They reject the beliefs that human bodies are shameful, or that physical pleasure is wrong. They believe that all acts of love and pleasure honor the gods and goddess.

"Gather you Witches in the night while the moon rides full. Gather you Witches in the darkness when the moon is hidden. Gather to follow the old ways, to drum, to sing, and to dance the ageless dance of life. Gather in a circle, man to woman, woman to man, in the circle of life as the goddess has taught you." Hope chanted as Tommy was laid upon the summit of the pentagram stones.

"Listen to the wind. Listen to the water. Listen to the fire. Listen to the Earth. Hear the heartbeat of the drums and the drumbeat of the heart." Hope continued. "Feel the power of the magic as it flows hand to hand around the circle."

Heather instructed the other young girls to remove Tommy's clothing while she facilitated his positioning.

He was laid out in the shape of an upside-down cross, upon the apex of the pentagram.

To the followers of the Old Religion, the pentagram is a symbol of the goddess Venus. It is also called the rose of Venus. It is an energetic symbol that creates a harmonizing field of negative ions around the human body to support and balance the body's natural magnetic field and aura. It is a psychological symbol that also corresponds to the human consciousness.

Venus is a morning star for two-hundred-sixty-six days. Corn takes two-hundred-sixty-six days to grow. Venus is an evening star for two-hundred-sixty-six days. The human gestation period is two-hundred-sixty-six days.

Heather had been the one who had been given the task of slashing Tommy's tire and placing the tracking device upon his vehicle. Though, she had no idea the consequences or chaos it would cause her family. Nor did she comprehend the overall effect it would have on her father's well-being. It had been the focal point when everything in her world had started to go wrong.

Her father's suicide had not been anticipated and she and her family had mourned and grieved over their loss.

However, to the Darkness, it was the timing of Michael's demise that was the most alarming. His death occurred out of sequence. He had threatened to expose the Coven and their practices. And he needed to be silenced. So, in order for the essence of his soul to be illuminated within the Old Religion, there had to be consistency. And there would need to be order. So, the darkness moved quickly.

Above all, the rules had to be adhered to. And his untimely death needed to be sanctified for an innocent soul to be taken.

And so, the darkness stepped in and made the correction.

"An innocent soul shall be taken. A shameless soul shall be chained." The Darkness spoke. "And a loving soul shall be free."

It was the way it had always been.

These were the rules of the darkness.

One soul should die innocently, representing the innocence of her baby's death. One soul should pay for the brutality and be incarcerated for life, in retribution for her baby's passing. And one soul, who loves her, should die willingly to symbolize atonement for the loss of her child.

There were always three. Rowan's death would complete the sacrificial trinity.

Tommy had been taken in the pouring rain, and his veins had been filled with the elixir of enlightenment. He would be allowed to remain aware of his surroundings, though his sight would appear as dreams, and he would not believe his mind.

Their father's blood had also been taken, and Tommy had been anointed in his life's blood. It was the way it should be …the way it had always been. And his hands had been placed upon the murder weapon, along the walls of their home, and upon its staircase railing.

"Gather you Witches in the circle and call upon the goddess and welcome her magic." Hope said. "Gather in the circle to celebrate the seasons of the Earth and the sacredness of life. Thank the goddess and encourage fertility so that our race will not perish." Hope continued. "Call forth the young ones, and welcome them to the ancient circle, and pass on the old ways to each new generation. Thus, has it been for a hundred thousand generations."

The fires raged and the flames rose high into the night sky, and the creatures that stood outside the light howled.

The sounds that filled the stillness were like that of wolves only maniacal, yipping sounds, screaming sounds and howls that resounded like words spoken in an ancient tongue.

And their eyes glowed with orange and amber.

"As a sign that you are truly free," Hope stated. "You shall be naked in your rites."

243

The twelve in robes shed their clothing and twelve youthful angelic female bodies embraced the winds and flickering flames as they stood around the fires. They were young. They were beautiful. And they were truly free.

"We are a part of nature." Hope continued. "And our bodies are as natural as the trees and the bears in the forest. Our clothes conceal much of our beauty. We choose to meet the moon and the wind with more of our skin and less of our raiment. For the breath of life is in the starlight and the hand of life is in the wind." Hope continued. "We are Sky-clad. We are clothed only by the sky. And forget not that the earth delights in the feel of our bare feet, and the winds long to play with the softness of our hair."

All acts of love and pleasure are rituals that honor the goddess. The union of male and female is the ultimate act of creation and is sacred and holy.

Sexuality is a powerful form of magic energy, and sexual union is the highest form of worship. There are no age limits or restrictions because there are no social moralities or religious restraints. Sexual magic, sacred sexuality and sexual behaviors are practiced within the coven circle without remorse, legalities or emotional entanglements regarding their sexuality.

"We honor the dark as well as the light." Hope said. "For the new moon is naught but the other side of the full moon." She continued. "The darkness loves us, and it

244

completes us and our tie to its power binds us to the earth's cycle of birth. Its divinity and ours is immanent."

As the flames danced and the beasts howled, the sisters of the Coven worshipped Tommy's body.

And the beasts howled and worked themselves …into a heated frenzy.

The tallest creature, the alpha-male, came out of the wood on all fours and traversed the grass and stone to the fire, and then he stood up-right, likened unto Man, beside the darkness within Tara. And he raised his long arms over his head and howled greatly. He was a massive creature, standing nearly eight feet tall. And he celebrated in the lust and the animalistic carnal human breeding.

The Darkness within Tara was standing, because she was not limited to the restraints of her injuries. She had long since developed the strength, the will, the magic and skills necessary to throw off the human bondage of her wheelchair. She could rise and walk beneath the heavens and the stars and amidst the shadows in the light.

Heather would take pictures of the created sexual magic within the Coven circle with Tommy's phone. The same photographs …that an unjust society would soon call deviant, disgraceful and perverse.

And after this night, Hope, the youngest high priestess to ever be honored by her Coven family with the title, would proudly carry …Tommy's baby.

"She is made of simple things." Hope said. "She is made of flowers and smiles, sunshine and kisses. She is made of music and stardust, moonlight, raindrops and wolves."

"To the winds that blow from the four corners of the Earth," The Coven chanted. "And unto the waters that bring life, please accept our offerings and our sacrifice this night. We evoke the elements of the earth, water, air and the flame, join us."

And they prayed to the angels, the goddess of nature and to the spirits of the air and the water and the trees.

♫ The world was on fire, and no one could save me but you. It's strange what desire will make foolish people do. I'd never dreamed that I'd meet somebody like you. And I'd never dreamed that I'd lose somebody like you. No, I don't want to fall in love. No, I don't want to fall in love with you. ♫

♫ What a wicked game you played to make me feel this way. What a wicked thing to do to let me dream of you. What a wicked thing to say you never felt this way. What a wicked thing to do to make me dream of you. And I don't want to fall in love. ♫ Wicked Game - Chris Isaak

to be continued.

An Author's Request

"I truly appreciate the time you gave to read this on-going story. And I would be ...incredibly grateful ...if you were to share your thoughts with me on Amazon. The story doesn't end with Tommy being locked away ...after all ...Hope is carrying his child ...and there is so much more to reveal. I love continuing this saga.

Please help me get more reviews. Tell your friends about this Novel and add your comments. The best reviews could possibly be included in the next addition to this series."

Tony

Made in the USA
Columbia, SC
16 November 2022

70994417R00152